He'd felt Cassie's body relax next to his as she slept.

But now she moved restlessly and gave a broken cry, awakening him.

He called her name, but whatever nightmare had her in its grasp wasn't ready to let go. "Cassie!" He shook her shoulder urgently, until finally her eyelids fluttered open. "How do you feel?"

She didn't look at him as she replied, "Fine. Just a dream. I've had it since I was a kid."

He noted the shakiness of her fingers as she pushed them through her hair. "What's it about?"

"Murder."

"Whose murder?"

She looked at him, and her eyes held horror in their depths. "Mine."

Dear Reader,

We keep raising the bar here at Silhouette Intimate Moments, and our authors keep responding by writing books that excite, amaze and compel. If you don't believe me, just take a look RaeAnne Thayne's *Nothing To Lose,* the second of THE SEARCHERS, her ongoing miniseries about looking for family—and finding love.

Valerie Parv forces a new set of characters to live up to the CODE OF THE OUTBACK in her latest, which matches a sexy crocodile hunter with a journalist in danger and hopes they'll *Live To Tell.* Kylie Brant's contribution to FAMILY SECRETS: THE NEXT GENERATION puts her couple *In Sight of the Enemy,* a position that's made even scarier because her heroine is pregnant—with the hero's child! Suzanne McMinn's amnesiac hero had *Her Man To Remember,* and boy, does *he* remember *her*—because she's the wife he'd thought was dead! Lori Wilde's heroine is *Racing Against the Clock* when she shows up in Dr. Tyler Fresno's E.R., and now his heart is racing, too. Finally, cross your fingers that there will be a *Safe Passage* for the hero and heroine of Loreth Anne White's latest, in which an agent's "baby-sitting" assignment turns out to be unexpectedly dangerous—and passionate.

Enjoy them all, then come back next month for more of the most excitingly romantic reading around—only in Silhouette Intimate Moments.

Yours,

Leslie J. Wainger
Executive Editor

Please address questions and book requests to:
Silhouette Reader Service
U.S.: 3010 Walden Ave., P.O. Box 1325, Buffalo, NY 14269
Canadian: P.O. Box 609, Fort Erie, Ont. L2A 5X3

In Sight of the Enemy

KYLIE BRANT

Silhouette®

INTIMATE MOMENTS™

Published by Silhouette Books

America's Publisher of Contemporary Romance

Special thanks and acknowledgment are given to Kylie Brant for her contribution to the FAMILY SECRETS: THE NEXT GENERATION series.

For Jordan, who thinks he's suffered greatly as the "middle child" but has really been spoiled beyond belief! We love you, honey.

Acknowledgments

Special thanks goes to Roxanne Rustand, for her expertise on horses and their behavior, and her unfailing support and friendship; to Vickie Taylor, fellow author, for generously sharing her experience and knowledge of the eastern Texas forests; and to my buddy, Paul Leavens, Director of Emergency Services, Mason City Mercy Hospital, for being my go-to guy every time I'm under deadline and need to shoot someone! I appreciate everyone's help more than I can say. Any mistakes in accuracy are the sole responsibility of the author.

SILHOUETTE BOOKS

ISBN 0-373-27393-2

IN SIGHT OF THE ENEMY

Visit Silhouette Books at www.eHarlequin.com

Printed in U.S.A.

KYLIE BRANT

lives with her husband and children. Besides being a writer, this mother of five works full-time teaching learning-disabled students. Much of her free time is spent in her role as professional spectator at her kids' sporting events.

An avid reader, Kylie enjoys stories of love, mystery and suspense—and she insists on happy endings. She claims she was inspired to write by all the wonderful authors she's read over the years. Now most weekends and all summer she can be found at the computer, spinning her own tales of romance and happily-ever-afters.

She invites readers to check out her online read in the reading room at eHarlequin.com. Readers can write to Kylie at P.O. Box 231, Charles City, IA 50616, or e-mail her at kyliebrant@hotmail.com. Her Web site address is www.kyliebrant.com.

FAMILY SECRETS: THE NEXT GENERATION

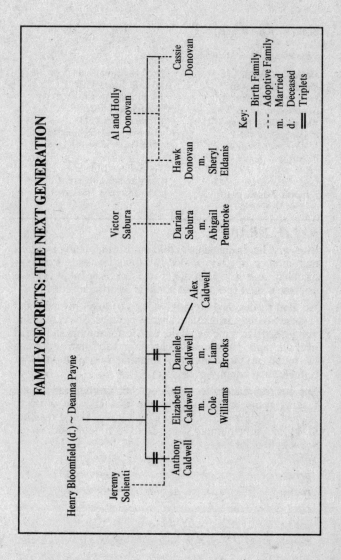

Henry Bloomfield (d.) ~ Deanna Payne

Jeremy Solienti

Anthony Caldwell

Elizabeth Caldwell m. Cole Williams

Danielle Caldwell m. Liam Brooks

Alex Caldwell

Victor Sabura

Darian Sabura m. Abigail Pembroke

Al and Holly Donovan

Hawk Donovan m. Sheryl Eldanis

Cassie Donovan

Key:
— Birth Family
--- Adoptive Family
m. Married
d. Deceased
≡ Triplets

Chapter 1

July

Cassie Donovan was dreaming of murder.

The familiar nightmare dragged her in, clutched her in its vicious grip, making escape impossible.

It was a familiar scene, one she'd experienced repeatedly throughout her life. Each time it was replayed for its audience of one with the same setting, the same characters. But rather than dulling its horror, repetition had honed it like a sharp blade.

The dark-haired woman in the room is packing quickly, frantically. Someone had painstakingly reproduced nineteenth-century splendor in the bedroom, but the panic in her movements is in marked contrast to the antiquated charm of her surroundings. Her yellow ruffled sundress flutters as she moves from dresser to suitcase, dropping a jumble of clothes into it. And then she looks up, an expression of terror on her face, listening to a sound that only she can hear. The lid to the suitcase is slammed shut, the locks engaged and the woman straightens, spine stiff with resolve or fear for the as yet unseen threat.

Cassie moved in the bed restlessly, her subconscious searching for means of escape. But there would be no avoiding the inevitable conclusion. Not for the woman in the bed. Not for the one in the dream.

She sends a quick look toward the half-closed closet door before grabbing the suitcase, carrying it down the hallway to a living room. A man clad in dark trousers and white shirt is already there. Slowly he rolls up his sleeves, first one, then the other. And though the woman lifts her chin, nerves show in the way her fingers tighten around the handle of the suitcase.

"Where are they?"

She doesn't back down in the face of his angry demand, although she has to be aware of the menace in it.

The pretty Tiffany lamp, with the delicate wisteria winding about the shade, is picked up, sails across the room. When the woman ducks, it shatters against the wall, shards of colored glass spraying like tiny missiles. And then the man lunges, diving for her and the woman dodges, dropping the suitcase. He catches the fabric of her dress, yanks her to the couch and his balled fist smashes into her face.

"Where are they?"

The words are uttered in an enraged roar, the blows raining down fierce and punishing. The woman fights, almost breaks free, but his hands go to her throat and squeeze. She claws at them in an attempt to loosen his grip, but his fingers tighten as reason recedes and temper takes over. Her struggles grow weaker, until finally her hands drop away, one palm facing upward in a silent supplication. And then there's no sound in the room but the harsh breathing of the man above her, his guttural furious cry.

Cassie gasped for air, her eyes flying open. She was only half-aware that she was on the floor, beside the bed, one hand flung up in a macabre reflection of the woman's position in the dream. For the next few seconds she concentrated on the simple act of hauling air into oxygen-starved lungs.

She rose awkwardly, then stumbled toward the window. The moon was hanging fat and full in the diamond-studded sky, but the sight failed to soothe her as it usually did. The aftereffects of the nightmare still prickled her skin, and she rubbed her arms to chase away the lingering chill.

The dream had come often enough over the years that it was etched in her memory like acid on glass. If she wanted to, she could call up every tiny detail. The decorative vase on the ornate oak dresser in the bedroom, filled with fragrant gardenias. The Tiffany lamp on the table in the living room, with its delicate flowered vines tracing across the shade. The cameo-backed couch, the polished tongue-and-groove wood floor. The terror and resolve of the woman. The horrible intent of the man.

But try as she might, she could never put a face to the murderer.

It wasn't until she was older that she'd recognized

the void and tried to fill it. But each time the dream
replayed, she was a helpless spectator. She could see
only the back of the man, from the shoulders down;
the width of the rooms; the woman engaged in her
last violent struggle for life.

But no, that wasn't quite true either. Because she
could "see" one thing that couldn't be explained by
visual acuity. Although the door to the room's closet
was almost closed, she knew there was a little dark-
haired boy huddled inside it, a baby's soft terry toy
clutched tightly in his hands. And she recognized that
there were two victims in that house. One who would
die and another whose end she'd never know.

For there wasn't a doubt in her mind that the
dream would come true. All of her dreams did.

Cassie didn't know how old she'd been before
she'd become aware of that inexplicable ability she'd
been born with. The first instance she could recall
she'd been about four and had dreamed every detail
of the colt her favorite mare would give birth to. The
events in the dreams that had followed over the years
had never failed to materialize. But tonight's nightmare had occurred with the most frequency.

With a hand that still shook she reached up, wiped
her clammy forehead. It was easy to guess what had
sparked it this time—the room in the bed-and-
breakfast where she'd just returned from spending
two days with her lover.

Shane had arranged the weekend away as a surprise for her, but her pleasure at his thoughtfulness
had died abruptly once they'd walked into their
room. When she'd viewed the turn-of-the-century
furnishings her blood had run thick and cold. Although not identical to those in the dream, they had

been similar enough to cause her a sleepless weekend. She'd tried, but she knew she hadn't been able to completely hide the strain it had taken. Which hadn't done a thing to heal the rift that was forming between Shane and herself.

Resting her forehead against the cool pane of glass, she closed her eyes. She shouldn't have to struggle to hide who she was, *what* she was, from the only man she'd ever allowed herself to love. Love—real love—meant acceptance, didn't it? But Shane hadn't reacted as she'd hoped when she'd tried to explain to him a few weeks ago about the dreams that sometimes came, unbidden. And he was nowhere close to believing that her precognition—or any psychic ability—was real. Especially not when she told him what she'd dreamed about him and his upcoming assignment for Doctors Without Borders.

Her twin brother, Hawk, would frown disapprovingly if he knew she'd been honest with Shane, but she couldn't fathom a future with a man she had to keep secrets from. And Shane hadn't rejected her when she'd told him about her ability. She opened her eyes to stare blindly out into the night, taking a measure of comfort from the thought. As dismayed as he'd been by her revelation, he hadn't walked away. But neither was he anywhere close to believing in it.

The weekend had been a chance for them to repair a relationship that had recently become more tenuous. Appreciation of Shane's gesture had kept her from suggesting a different place to stay. Had kept her from falling into a deep sleep while there, lest tonight's nightmare make an appearance. But all she'd managed, in the end, was to delay it.

She gave a little sigh, her breath fogging the window. Rubbing at the condensation absently, she pushed aside the trepidation filling her. The two of them would work through this. *They would.* What they had was too rare to give up on so easily. He just needed time to adjust, and she could grant him that time. As long as he reached some sort of acceptance in the end.

Turning back toward the room, she stared at the rumpled bedcovers with a renewed sense of dread. She wasn't ready to crawl back in that bed again. Not while it still took such effort to keep the mental door closed tightly against those all-too familiar images.

But like sneaky fingers of fog, remnants of the dream filtered through her memory, leaving an icy wake. Her bedroom should be a haven. Certainly it couldn't have been further removed from the one in the nightmare. She'd always deliberately embraced more contemporary furnishings, and the ranch bore her stamp of Southwestern decor. There was nothing fussy or overtly feminine about her bedroom trappings, or her wardrobe. Her clothing favored function and tailoring over frills and ruffles. There wasn't a hint of the softly feminine touches apparent in the room from the dream.

But despite the effort she'd taken to avoid such similarities, she knew that her efforts would be in vain. Over the years she'd learned to accept the inevitability of the dreams. She could no more prevent them than she could change their events from coming true. There was no doubt that the woman in tonight's nightmare would eventually die a violent, hideous death. There could be no evading it.

She hugged herself with her arms, in an attempt to control the shudders that worked through her. A familiar sense of fatalism filled her. Because although Cassie couldn't identify the setting or the time in the dream, the woman's face was all too familiar. She saw it every time she looked in the mirror.

For as long as she could remember, she'd been dreaming of her own inescapable murder.

Dr. Shane Farhold shifted on his bench seat in the stadium, his gaze flicking over his surroundings idly. Jean-clad men and casually dressed women packed the outdoor arena. Regardless of gender, a full half of the occupants wore Stetsons, and most carried beers afforded by the vendors in the place. It would be hard to imagine a scene further removed from those in his former home in Boston, and the differences were satisfying. After his mother's death there had seemed little reason to stay in the city. And once his only remaining family had found him again, he'd had every reason to leave.

With an ease born of long practice he shoved that memory aside and concentrated on the voice on the loudspeaker announcing the next contestant in the Bareback Bronc contest. Cassie was up next. As if on cue, his stomach clenched in tight knots. He could use a scalpel to slice open a man's chest without a moment's hesitation, but the sight of Cassie on a huge unbroken horse always had the power to turn his blood to ice. He knew all too well just how many bones could break if a person hit the ground with just the right amount of force. He'd pointed that out to her once and she'd only laughed and said that was why she preferred to stay on the back of the horse.

The gate on the chute swung open. There was a split second of stillness, as if the huge roan was transfixed by the crowd. Then it exploded out of the chute, a whirling dervish of clashing hooves.

"Relax, Doc," said the bearded man beside Shane. "She marked out just fine. Always does."

He didn't bother to correct the man. His concern was hardly on whether or not Cassie's feet had been placed above the break of the horse's shoulder on its first jump out of the chute. Her dainty form atop the furious horse looked spectacularly out of place. The eight-second clock crawled with excruciating slowness, a marked contrast to the frenzied movements of the animal.

Cassie was smiling widely, looking as though she was having the time of her life. The rigging grasped in one hand, her other was raised in the air to avoid accidentally touching the horse or her equipment, an automatic disqualification. The animal reared then spun, engaging in a series of staccato, teeth-jarring sideways jumps.

She looked, to Shane, to be spurring in perfect rhythm with the horse's movements. If the crowd's roar of approval was any indication, they agreed. The final couple seconds were a blur, with the animal spinning and bucking wildly. When the buzzer sounded, however, Cassie was still seated, her smile still bright as the pickup men rode out to secure the horse.

Releasing the rigging, she reached over to one of the pickup horses and transferred to it. The horse veered free of the bronc and Cassie slid off its back, turned in Shane's direction and blew him a kiss before running out of the arena.

Relief mingled with a sort of amused irritation. The man next to Shane guffawed and elbowed him. "What'd I tell you? Cassie knows what she's doin'. There's no one knows horses better'n her and Hawk Donovan." He then fell silent, listening intently as the announcer stated her scores and the crowd applauded once again.

Minutes later, Cassie was slipping into the seat next to his, accepting the congratulations and good-natured ribbing of those around her with equanimity. She went into his arms with an ease that never failed to warm him. "I didn't catch the score, did you?" When Shane repeated it for her, she wrinkled her nose and shook her head.

"What?" he asked. "That's a great score. Best so far."

"With eight more contestants after me, it won't be good enough to win." She settled in the seat next to his. "Half the score is based on the horse's performance, and with my weight I'm never going to be exposed to the horse's maximum strength."

She could still surprise him, despite the fact they'd been dating six months. "If you know that going in, why the heck do you take the risks?"

Her lips curved. "For the thrill, of course." She laughed when she saw his expression. "You know what else would thrill me?"

Her tone was innocent enough. The hand sliding up his leg was anything but. He clamped one hand firmly over hers to stop her teasing, even as his hormones expressed immediate interest. He wasn't yet entirely comfortable with just how easily he responded to this woman. "What?"

"Letting you take me out of here and..." She leaned closer to breathe the rest into his ear. "...buy me a corn dog."

Shane winced. "Do you know what they put in those things?"

"No, and don't ruin it for me. We can't come to the county fair without tasting all the once-a-year treats."

He rose and followed her out of the stands. "Okay, but I'm not buying cotton candy. I do have medical ethics to uphold, you know."

Slipping her arm through his, she leaned her head on his arm. "No problem. I brought my own money."

Shane leaned back on the one empty bench they managed to find in the crowded midway and stretched out his legs. Crossing his arms over his stomach, he barely managed to stifle a groan. Despite his best intentions, he hadn't done particularly well at withstanding Cassie's constant invitations to take "just a bite." As a result, he'd ingested some of the most dubious offerings masquerading as food he'd ever experienced. Following her gaze to a nearby food cart, he said emphatically, "Don't even think about it. After three corn dogs—which could be more aptly named heart attack on a stick—cotton candy, a pretzel, a caramel apple and something called wild melon sorbet, you can't possibly be thinking of eating a funnel cake."

With a look of unmistakable regret on her face,

she nodded. "You're right. I should give it another hour. I'll be hungry again by then."

He cocked an eyebrow, raked her slight figure with disbelief. "Your metabolism just might constitute a medical miracle. I should alert researchers at the National Institute of Health."

Quick reflexes had him deflecting the elbow she jabbed at him. "Not everything has a scientific explanation, you know. And my metabolism is only one of my inexplicable talents."

Her words managed to puncture his feeling of well-being. He didn't want to engage in yet another conversation about her so-called abilities. Not for the first time he wondered what had happened to the woman he'd thought he'd known. The one full of life and fun, but with shadows of secret sorrows in her eyes that she'd never spoken of. The one whose sudden claim of psychic ability terrified and dismayed him by turns.

Deliberately, he changed the subject. "What's the game plan for the rest of the afternoon? Are you signed up for any more death-defying events?"

She laughed, shook her head. "Nope, but you really haven't experienced the fair until you enter something yourself. I think they're still looking for contestants for the pie-eating contest."

Apparently the expression on his face was its own answer. She went on without pausing a beat. "No? Well, the longest beard is out, because even if you'd been interested, you didn't get the head start most of those guys did. Although," she reached up, rubbed her hand over his unshaven jaw, "I have to say, the day-old beard is a good look for you." Her fingers lingered, and her touch, coupled with the slow smile she gave him, ignited an immediate flicker of heat.

"Really?" He lowered his voice intimately. "That's not what you said when my whiskers were leaving marks on your skin yesterday morning. I distinctly remember when I was kissing your breasts and you said—"

"Or we could go see Hawk at the horse barn." Cassie jumped up, her cheeks flushed. "I probably should. He's been stuck with the chores all day."

Shane rose as well, satisfied by the flare of color his suggestive remark had brought to her face. The woman was a study of contrasts. Strong and confident in her reputation as one of the leading horse breeders in the nation, yet appearing almost unsure sometimes of the allure of her own femininity. Assertive on one hand, with flashes of an unexpected vulnerability that had gotten to him from the first. Discovering the layers of her was an endless fascination.

Or had been until he'd uncovered the one thing about her that would have sent him running from any other woman. The one thing that he'd never be able to live with.

An innate protectiveness had him moving closer to her side, to shield her from the mob of people jostling around them as they made their way to the horse barn. He couldn't explain to himself why he hadn't run, couldn't explain the stubborn hope he clung to that he could talk her out of her sudden foolishness. He only knew it was imperative that he do so.

The crowd thinned as they got closer to their destination. Cassie's steps slowed as they approached a line of children having their faces painted by an older woman sitting on a stool at the edge of the midway. There were shrieks of laughter as the children dodged around them on their way back to their waiting parents, eager to show off the small brightly colored pictures adorning their cheeks.

"Well, this seems like a harmless enough interest," he said, glancing down at her. She'd come to a complete halt, her gaze fixed on the woman with the paints. "Are you getting the lasso or the horse?"

Her head cocked, Cassie stared intently at the woman. "She looks familiar, but I don't think I know her, and I recognize just about most in the county."

Shane shrugged. The sun overhead was merciless in a way he'd been unfamiliar with until he'd experienced Texas heat firsthand. He found himself wondering if the horse barn would be air-conditioned. Somehow he doubted it.

"Maybe she's someone who travels the county fairs in the area," he suggested.

At that moment, the older woman looked up and smiled. "Come, Cassie, it's your turn now."

There was a slight accent to her words that Shane couldn't identify, but it matched the exotic slant of her eyes. Aside from that, her appearance blended in with most of the other fairgoers. She was dressed in jeans, boots and a short-sleeved denim shirt. Her long dark hair was streaked with white, and she wore it pulled back in a simple ponytail.

Cassie smiled tentatively and walked toward the lady. "I'm sorry. I feel like I should know you."

"You know a great many things, not all of which can be explained. But you trust in your gift, as you should. You'll share that ability with one to come, and teach her to nurture it. As you must. The ability that brings you your greatest sadness will also save your life.''

Shane felt, rather than saw, the jolt the words had on Cassie. And he'd heard as much cryptic nonsense from the stranger as he wanted to. ''C'mon, Cass,'' he said shortly. ''I thought you wanted to go see Hawk.''

But she remained rooted to the ground, her gaze on the woman before her. If she'd heard him, she gave no sign of it. The older lady leaned forward, a slight lilt to her voice. ''Your daughter will share your gift and you will teach her to use it well, not hide it as you've been forced to. Accept your future without the fear you're used to regarding it with. There is joy there, as well as sorrow.''

''My daughter? But when…''

Irritation turned to something else. His hand went to Cassie's back, in an effort to move her away. ''Lady, this fortune-telling nonsense might play with the rest of the fairgoers, but you picked the wrong couple to lay it on.'' He couldn't believe his damnable luck. All Cassie needed right now was a stranger's babblings to encourage her in her own ridiculous notions.

Her attention switched to him. ''It is you, Shane, who regards it as nonsense, but you must learn to listen, and to accept. Cassie's fear for you is well founded. Afghanistan holds dangers for you that cannot be comprehended. Consider well before deciding your course. Your decision will change everything.''

There was a moment of stunned shock before fury

began to boil. He looked at Cassie, a bitter sense of betrayal almost choking him. "No wonder she looks familiar to you. How long did it take for the two of you to cook this thing up?"

Cassie stared at him, a mask of confusion on her face. "What? Shane, this only proves what I've been trying to tell you. I knew you shouldn't go on that assignment. It isn't too late. You could still back out."

He took a step away from her. And then another. It was safer that way, given the rage surging through him. "Someone more easily controlled might even fall for this scene. Of course, a more honest woman would never have set up such an elaborate ruse to manipulate a man, but hey, whatever means necessary, right?"

Hurt mingled with determination in her expression, but he wasn't going to allow it to affect him. Not when it appeared that he'd been the biggest fool of all time. Had he given it a thought, he would have found it ironic that the greatest betrayals in his life had been perpetuated by frauds and fakes who'd pretended to love him.

But he wasn't much in the mood to appreciate the irony.

"Shane, you have to listen." There was desperation in Cassie's voice, in the clutch of her fingers when she laid them on his arm. "If you go through with that assignment, I'm afraid you may not come home alive. I told you about my dream—"

He jerked away from her touch. "You told me. What you didn't tell me was the lengths you'd go to get your own way."

"This isn't about me! It's about—"

"Finally something we can agree on." His jaw was tight, his chest felt as if a vise squeezed it. "This isn't about you at all. Not anymore."

The older woman was speaking again, but he couldn't hear her. There was a roaring in his ears, and a fist punching his heart as he turned to leave. The first step felt like a surgical slice, neatly peeling away a part of his life he'd begun to think of as permanent. With the second step, a blessed sort of numbness settled in and he welcomed it, even knowing it wouldn't last. The lack of feeling made it possible to take the next step. And then the next. Soon he was striding rapidly toward the parking lot where he'd left his vehicle. Away from the charlatan spouting her cryptic psychic nonsense.

And away from the only woman he'd ever loved.

Chapter 2

Three months later

Shane pushed open the door of his house and was immediately assailed by the dual odors of Pine-Sol and stale air. Although his housecleaner had been instructed to keep the place clean in his absence, she'd obviously neglected to air it out regularly.

He walked through the entryway to drop the bundle of mail he'd collected from the Post Office, then went back to the porch to retrieve his bags. He set them down in the hallway, nudging them out of the way with one foot. Leaving the door open, he went back to deal with the mail that had accumulated in his absence.

The place felt foreign, distant somehow. Which was amazing, considering the places he'd been living for the past several months.

Living. That was the operative word. He'd come back to the States alive. There had been times he'd been convinced that would never happen.

Without any real interest, he began sorting through the mail. Half of it was junk, which he set aside to be discarded later. There was an oddly disorienting feeling to be reading advertisements guaranteeing financial success, and catalogs featuring malnourished, scantily clad models, when only twenty hours earlier he'd been in a country where a man was routinely killed for the dollar in his pocket or the half-worn boots on his feet. Where a baby died for lack of ample penicillin. Where the medications that could save lives were bartered by warlords and thieves as lucrative items on a thriving black market.

Like a flick of a switch he turned that memory off and concentrated on the task at hand. Three piles— for junk, professional and personal. The latter was woefully thin, consisting of only a letter that looked to be from his lawyer. Until… His hand faltered when he came upon the plain white envelope without a return address. He didn't need one. He recognized the handwriting.

Cassie's.

A memory of her face flashed into his mind, its appearance a bit too easily summoned for comfort. With slightly more difficulty, he pushed the mental image aside. She was out of his life. Had been for three months. Nothing contained in the message would change that.

He let the letter drop from his fingers to land on the top of the third pile, and continued sorting. The wound in his shoulder had stiffened up on the plane and throbbed dully. The bandage needed to be changed, and he'd have to get a new prescription now that he was home. Somehow he couldn't summon the interest or inclination to do any of that at the moment.

The phone rang, the sound startling in the silence of the house. Shane answered it and, upon hearing the voice on the other end, felt his blood go glacial.

"Shane? Oh, thank the goddesses. Where have you been?"

"Gran." His voice was flat. "How did you find me?"

He could almost picture the careless wave of her hand. "Oh, that doesn't really matter, does it, sweetie? What matters is that you're finally home. Someone at the hospital where you work told me that you were out of the country. Did you enjoy your vacation? I always worry about your working too hard."

Shane's mouth twisted wryly. "The *vacation* was fine. What do you want?"

Her voice went persuasive. "Now, dear, don't sound like that. I just wanted to say hello, that's all. Family should keep in touch, and with your dear mother gone we need each other more than ever."

"Difficult to figure, considering I never needed you at all." He looked at his reflection in the mirror hanging above the hall table. A stranger stared back at him. Hair that hadn't been cut in months, three days' growth of beard on his face, partially hiding a fresh scar that began beneath his chin and zigzagged down three inches to the right. Surface changes, for the most part, with the exception of his eyes. Ghosts lurked there, haunted fragments of memory that he doubted he'd ever shake. But for all the changes, he was still Dr. Shane Farhold.

He just wasn't certain who that man was anymore.

"Shane? Are you still there?"

"Yes." With a mental jerk, he shifted his attention back to the woman on the other end of the line and answered her question.

"Well, that's good, then. I wanted to tell you about the sweetest little shop I've set up. I'm selling Wiccan items and teaching some classes. You can't believe the response I've gotten. With my ability for summoning the spirits, there's a never-ending stream of people who are lonely for a long departed loved one. But not all people are open-minded about that, as you recall."

He read the underlying message in what she didn't say. "Run a little afoul of the local law, did you?"

Her tone was just right. A little bewildered, with a touch of the shakiness one might expect in a seventy-year-old woman. Except that Genevieve Fleming had never exuded signs of her age in her entire life. She didn't admit to it at all, unless it could help her in some way. "They're hounding me, Shane, treating me like some common criminal. They want a payoff, of course, a bribe to leave me alone to conduct my business in peace."

"Really." When he noticed his fist clenching, he consciously relaxed it, continued sorting the mail. "Are you sure it's a bribe they want, Gran? I believe it's more commonly referred to as bail."

There was a moment of silence, while she rapidly regrouped, but only a moment. She'd always been quick to recover. Quick to assess any situation and milk it for all she was worth. Then she gave a martyred sigh, like a woman trying her best to be strong. "You have caller ID, I suppose. Well, as a matter of fact, I hadn't wanted to alarm you, but for some reason I've been put in jail. I don't know how to handle this. I feel so alone." Her voice broke.

There had been a time, even a few months ago, when the sound would have tugged at his conscience. Guilt was a habit decades in the making, difficult to break. But right now he felt nothing. No guilt. No compassion. Nothing but a weary sort of irritation that he might have felt for a particularly annoying stranger. His grandmother was little more than that, at any rate.

"Considering your experience with jails around the country, it's hard to believe you're totally out of your element." He tossed a credit card application onto the discard pile. "You have my lawyer's number. Use it."

"He hasn't been helpful at all. Do you know, he expects me to plead guilty? If he was really worth the money you pay him, he'd post my bail and have the charges dismissed. He refuses to get me out of here."

"Because you've skipped bail the last two times you've been arrested," he reminded her. "Leaves us in a rather uncomfortable position when you can't be depended on to show up for the court date." His gaze dropped once more to the plain white envelope, its very simplicity inviting him to pick it up. Open it. To delve once again into a morass of emotion that he was reluctant to repeat. There was something to be said for the lack of feeling he'd been experiencing for the past few weeks. Absence of emotion also meant absence of pain. One of those damn silver linings the Pollyanna types always talked about. If he had an ounce of self-preservation left, he'd toss the letter away with the junk mail.

"Shane, if you'd just fly here to talk to me, I'm sure we could work this out. I need to see my only grandchild." Genevieve's voice quavered a bit. "Remember when you lived with me what a great team we made? We were inseparable."

He smiled humorlessly. "Actually, I do remember teaming up with you. I remember *everything.* Which is why I have no interest in a reunion. I'd recommend that you call my lawyer and follow his advice. There's nothing more I can do." He was disconnecting the phone with one hand, even as he picked up Cassie's letter with the other.

He could think of no better time to read her letter than right after dealing with his grandmother. They had, after all, so much in common. With any luck he could dispense with Cassie's message as easily, as emotionlessly, as he had with Genevieve.

But that hope was dashed when he read the single line printed on the page.

We need to talk.

There was nothing else. Just four words followed by her neat signature. Nothing to hint at her reasons for contacting him. Certainly their last fight, a few days after the fair, had been passionately final.

We need to talk.

They'd said everything they needed to each other then, and, if truth be told, even more. When he remembered the bitterness with which they parted, regret surged, forging through the shield he'd erected around his heart. But as often as he'd turned it over in his mind, he'd never been able to figure another way for them.

He looked at the postmark on the envelope. It had been mailed after he'd been in Afghanistan for two months. His original assignment had been for four weeks, but he'd made arrangements to extend it. And then he had ended up staying even longer than he could have imagined.

His gaze dropped to the letter again. Whatever she wanted to talk to him about had already waited a month. Maybe she'd written the note in a weak moment, driven by memories and remorse. Perhaps she'd thought better of the missive as soon as it was mailed. At any rate, what would they talk about? If there was one thing he'd learned in the past few months, it was that regret never changed anything. What was done was done. And then one just figured out how to live with the results.

We need to talk.

He didn't need to talk to Cassie. He didn't need her on any level. He'd spent three long months learning that. What he needed at this moment was to contact the hospital, get himself back on rotation. To unpack and deal with his wash. Get some medical supplies, including a prescription of painkillers and maybe, if the mood struck him, a haircut so he wouldn't scare his patients. Those were his priorities right now, and every one of them could be accomplished without dredging up painful feelings that were better left safely buried.

Decision made, he balled the note up in his hand, let it drop to the floor and headed out the door.

* * *

Cassie murmured soothingly to the half-wild stallion, not attempting to move any closer to it. Its rolling eyes and flared nostrils told her exactly how agitated it was. Now she'd see how much she'd taught it about trust.

Her hand inched upward a fraction of an inch at a time, even as she kept up a running litany of calming sounds. Her gaze never left the animal's eyes. That was where she'd see its reaction first.

It whickered nervously, backed up a little, flicked its tail. She moved forward a step and it went still, warning her. She froze, but never stopped her low, soothing monologue. The horse shook its mane and danced sideways, then finally lowered its head and pricked its ears, watching her.

Recognizing that the timing was right, Cassie reached out slowly, stroking its shoulder before easing forward to rub its neck. When it lowered its head further, she snapped a lead rope on the halter and led it quietly toward the hands waiting in the barn's entrance.

"Damn if I know how she does it." Lonny, their newest and youngest hand, shook his head. "He was as spooked as I've ever seen him."

"He's been off his feed," Cassie frowned consideringly. "Maybe we should get the vet out here to give him a going-over. He could be coming down with a virus."

Jim reached out to take the lead rope and Cassie stepped back. "You're getting as good at that as Hawk, Cass."

She laughed. "No one's as good as Hawk when it comes to communicating with animals. But I've picked up a thing or two from him."

"You've put in a long day. Why don't you knock off?" The older man handed the horse off to Lonny, who led it away.

Gritting her teeth, Cassie mentally counted to ten before returning evenly, "I'm okay."

In his forties, Jim Burnhardt was their senior hand, and an invaluable help around the ranch. But he'd gotten into the habit of watching over her like a mama over her chicks in her brother's absence. Which told her, better than words, that her brother had specifically instructed him to do so.

Jim faced her again, eyeing her shrewdly. "When's Hawk coming home, anyway?"

"We spoke a few days ago, but he didn't say when he was returning." Removing his hat, Jim slicked his hand through his hair. "I was planning on going to town for more feed, but if you're going to work some more, I can stick around."

You'd think, Cassie thought aggrievedly, that she hadn't been working alongside the ranch hands since she was ten. Not for the first time, she wished she could give her brother a swift kick for making everyone around here suddenly see her as an invalid. "Go ahead and pick up the feed. The hardware store called, too, and the rolls of barbed wire we ordered are in. If you leave now, it's still going to be close to dark before you can get back. Why don't you just go straight home from town. You can bring the supplies with you tomorrow morning."

Jim hesitated, clearly torn between the logic of her suggestion and a misdirected sense of responsibility. "That makes sense, but…are you done outside here for the day, then?"

Patience, never her strong suit, abruptly splintered.

"For Pete's sake, Jim, I'm more than capable of—"
One look at the man's stoic countenance had her biting off the rest of her sentence. It was clear from his expression that her outburst wasn't going to change his mind, and he wasn't the one she needed to convince, at any rate. Hawk was behind this new suffocating mantle of protectiveness all the ranch hands had donned in his absence. Snapping at Jim wasn't going to change that.

"Fine." Her surrender wasn't managed with particular graciousness. "Tell Lonny and the others they can leave once the chores are done. I'll go concentrate on paperwork."

"That's good, then," Jim said, plainly relieved. "You probably have plenty of that with the Green-laurel Horse Sale coming up."

The fact that he was right didn't make her feel any better as she headed from the corral to the house. She much preferred spending her time engaged in physical labor. The trouble with paperwork was that it left the mind too much time to think. And those thoughts all too frequently focused on the one man she'd loved, then lost.

At least, she consoled herself, he was alive. The county rumor mill was alive and in good working order. She'd heard Shane was headed home, but details of his health had been maddeningly spare.

She took off her boots in the mudroom before heading through the kitchen toward the den. She'd spent more than a few months caught with emotions swinging wildly between hope and despair. There had been a finality to their last scene that was only partially owed to their breakup. Despite his refusal to believe her, she'd known what he'd been heading toward when he left for Afghanistan.

She just hadn't known if he'd come back alive.

The dream she'd had about his assignment there had been maddeningly incomplete, a collage of hazy snippets bursting with violence. The shot ringing out in the dead of night...the blood pouring from his body as it tumbled out of the jeep to the ground...

Living for months with those images branded on her mind would be enough to cause stress for anyone. And more than ever she was convinced that the recent changes in her health were due to just that: stress. She'd neither eaten nor slept well following Shane's departure. The waiting had been agonizing. Surely that was enough to explain the sudden lapses in thought she'd been experiencing the past couple months; the short interruptions in concentration and speech that had gotten Hawk increasingly concerned. Especially after it happened while she was working with the stallions.

She walked to the den and, with a sigh, settled in behind the large desk. She and her twin brother despised paperwork equally, and when he was around, they split the workload. But in his absence, she was forced to shoulder his share as well as her own. It wasn't a chore she relished.

It was unusual for Hawk to leave the ranch for any amount of time. But when the doctors in Greenlaurel had been unable to come up with a reason for her condition, he'd been determined to find one himself. He'd undertaken the search for their birth mother with the express purpose of discovering something, anything, in their genetic history that would help treat Cassie's condition.

And he'd been successful, for the most part. He'd managed to trace their birth mother, who was long deceased. He'd even, to her amazement, discovered they had a brother, a triplet, who she'd yet to meet. He'd been stingy with the details. But he had found notes that indicated their mother had experienced spells much like Cassie's. He'd called Cassie a few days earlier with a recipe for a tea that helped with the worst of the symptoms. The organic drink had accomplished what the endless round of medical tests and medications had failed to do. Unfortunately, she couldn't convince the hired help of that fact.

An hour went by, and then another. Cassie took a break for a quick dinner of soup and a salad before trudging back to the den. If she stayed at it until bedtime, she'd just about be caught up. With any luck, that would mean she wouldn't have to do more paperwork until right before the sale, which would be in another ten days. And by that time, Hawk would be home and she just might be able to guilt him into believing it was his turn at the desk.

The Greenlaurel Horse Sale was becoming a major source of income for the ranch. As their reputation as breeders of horses for dressage and jumping had grown, they'd had to do less and less traveling around the country, finding instead that potential buyers were seeking them out. The local sale gave them an avenue to showcase their stock and to place orders. Their sale bills had been circulating for months. Local motels in the area were fully booked for the date. And although Hawk had been vague about when he was returning home, there wasn't a doubt in Cassie's mind that he'd arrive well before the event.

She was almost finished double-checking the files

on each of the horses they were offering for sale when her fingers faltered, then stilled. A kaleidoscope of colors wheeled past her eyes and her heart began to pound. There was a sensation of speed, as if she were hurtling along atop a locomotive, her surroundings a blur. And then just as abruptly the sensations faded, leaving only brief, fragmented flashes in their wake. The bits formed a confusing mural of images that shifted and swirled before gradually settling into a recognizable form.

When the mental fog lifted, she looked around, disoriented. The first thing she saw was the tea she'd mixed with her dinner and carried in here, unfinished. With a hand that still shook, she reached for the glass, raised it to her lips and sipped.

The glass was set back on the desk and Cassie rolled her chair back, troubled. She hadn't had an episode since Hawk had given her this recipe, their birth mother's recipe, to try. Twice a day she mixed it, drinking it with breakfast and dinner. She'd missed her second dose only by a couple hours, and the symptoms had not only returned, but intensified.

She took a deep breath. Well, it wasn't the end of the world. At least she knew now how important it was to stay on schedule with the mixture. She waited a couple more minutes until her pulse had slowed, before getting up to go to the front door. The bell rang a moment before she reached it, as she'd known it would. And when she pulled the door open, she recognized the strangers standing before her. She'd "seen" them five minutes earlier.

"Cassie Donovan?"

The woman who spoke wore her dark hair long, with no attempt made to disguise the gray in it. She looked to be in her forties, but given the care she took with her appearance, was probably older. There was a look of competence about her, and a shrewd calculation in her eyes.

"I'm Cassie." Although her tone was friendly enough, she made no move to unlock the screen door between them. Dusk was rapidly approaching, and the place was isolated. Cassie had never feared staying alone at the ranch, but she'd been raised to be aware of the dangers, and took precautions.

"I'm Darla Billings. This is my husband Stan." Cassie glanced at the large man beside her and thought they made an odd couple. He was bulky with a muscular build that was owed more to pumping iron than to the physical labor found on a ranch. His complexion was ruddy, his blond hair slicked back and his gray gaze inscrutable.

"This is unforgivably rude of us, I know." At the woman's rueful voice, Cassie's attention shifted back to her. "We drove from Kentucky, intending to visit family and then come to Greenlaurel for the horse sale. But since we were passing so close, I couldn't resist stopping by and seeing whether it would be possible to take a peek at your stock. We've been poring over your sale bill for weeks and I'm determined to take at least a couple Donovan Ranch mares back with me."

"I'm sorry, we don't do prior sales," Cassie said.

"Oh, we understand that." The woman hastened to add. "We just want to be able to narrow down our bidding list so we can concentrate on the stock that really interests us."

Cassie hesitated. It was an unusual request, but she was well aware of the lengths some people would go to get an advantage over others. And it seemed harmless enough. "Well...maybe you could come back tomorrow. There's not much daylight left." Innate caution prevented her from mentioning that her crew had left for the day. There was a niggling sense of discomfort that might have been left over from her earlier flash of this scene. Whatever its source, she had no intention of giving them a tour of the barns this evening.

"We'll be on the road again tomorrow." Stan spoke for the first time, his voice gravelly, as if from disuse. "Darla's folks live in New Mexico and we're heading there at dawn. We won't get back until the night before the sale."

"I'm not sure I—" Cassie stopped midsentence as she looked beyond the couple's Dodge pickup to the thin column of dust rising from the lane leading to the ranch. "Well, it looks like this is my night for company."

Both turned to look at the vehicle approaching from a distance. They exchanged a quick glance before facing her again. "I'm sorry, we don't want to keep you from your guests. Maybe we will come back tomorrow." When the man at her side seemed about to speak, Darla went on firmly, "Now, Stan, it's not going to matter if we head to Clayton a few hours later than planned." The car in the lane drew closer. As if in a sudden hurry to leave, the couple on the porch headed for the steps and began to descend them.

"I'd be glad to show you around if you can make time tomorrow," Cassie said politely. Whoever was heading for the ranch had just done her a favor. The newcomer's arrival had convinced the couple to leave, whereas she had been experiencing a decided lack of success. The two got back in their pickup, the woman driving. With a casual wave, she backed up the vehicle and drove away.

Cassie swung the door shut, a bit relieved. More than likely the new arrival would be Jim. He'd probably decided to drop off the supplies tonight rather than waiting until tomorrow as she'd suggested. If that was the case, it was doubtful he'd even come up to the house.

As she headed back to the den, she considered the spell she'd had prior to the strangers' arrival. The unexpected lapses in thought and activity had worried Hawk enough. But when they'd been followed by these flashes into the immediate future, he'd been driven to act. Had her mother possessed psychic ability, too, she wondered, or had she used the tea recipe only as a means to alleviate the other symptoms they shared? She was eager for Hawk to return home so she could get the answers to these and a multitude of other questions that had plagued her since their last conversation. Her brother wasn't exactly a chatterbox under the best of circumstances, but on the phone he was even more reticent than usual.

She'd lived with precognition all her life. But always before, her ability had manifested itself when her defenses were down and her subconscious took over. The dreams she had foretold events days, weeks or, in the case of the most frequent one, years in the future. She didn't understand why that would change now, and other than Hawk, there was no one she could discuss it with.

Cassie gave a little laugh as she imagined sharing that little tidbit with the medical staff at Greenlaurel

Community Hospital. They'd have her fitted for a straitjacket and safely ensconced in a padded room in record time. Her brother had been right. No one else could know about her ability. Other people didn't, wouldn't, understand. She'd discovered that the hard way.

The doorbell rang again, and Cassie turned back to the door, puzzled. Jim always went to the side door, so she must have been wrong in assuming her visitor was her foreman. With a sliver of apprehension she went to the door, opened it. Then stood frozen in shock when she recognized the man standing before her.

Shane. A dizzying wave of joy hit her, followed by relief, concern and then apprehension again. Her stomach clenched, tying into tight, neat knots, and her mind went abruptly blank. Now that the time had come, she had absolutely no idea what to say to him.

"Are you going to let me in?" His voice was perhaps the most familiar thing about him. Certainly there was nothing in his hard expression that reminded her of the tender lover who had held her in his arms. But given their acrimonious parting, she shouldn't be surprised.

The memory of that final scene was enough to have her spine stiffening. Shoving aside any softer memories, she unlatched the screen door, held it open.

"I heard you just returned. I didn't expect to see you so soon."

She stepped aside as he walked into the house, careful to avoid touching him. She didn't need to be assailed by familiar memories, to have old feelings rushing back to taunt her with what had been. She

didn't need to realize that the attraction burned just
as brightly as it had three months ago. And every bit
as futilely.

When she turned from closing the door, he was
facing her, one hand jammed in his jeans pocket.
Hungrily her gaze moved over him, taking inventory.
He was leaner, harder. She looked at his chest, but
could see no signs of the injury she knew was hidden
beneath his clothes. The jagged scar that worked
down the side of his throat made her heart lurch. And
then her gaze rose, to rest on his eyes. The eyes of
a stranger, one who'd been to hell and back and
hadn't yet adjusted to the journey.

"I don't know why I came," he said harshly. "We
said all we had to say before I left."

Anger, a quick violent surge of it, flared through
her, like a comet blazing a path through the night
sky. "Your brush with death obviously didn't teach
you tolerance."

He stared at her for a moment, then shook his
head. "You talked to Simon at the hospital?"

"All he said was that you were coming home,"
she said simply.

He considered her for a moment longer. His friend
Simon Thurson was the only person Shane had given
even the sketchiest details of his experiences to. Finally he shrugged. "I don't know what you heard
about my injuries, but I'm fine." At least he would
be, once he'd slept for about three days and regained
some more mobility in his shoulder. With any luck,
he could be back in the operating room within a couple weeks.

Her mouth twisted. "You're far from fine, Shane.
But if you're convinced, who am I to argue?" She

went past him to the couch and sat. He remained where he was. With the remarkable clarity of hindsight he realized he shouldn't have come. It wasn't like him to entertain himself by pulling scabs off barely healed wounds. And the wound caused by their breakup was every bit as painful as the injury in his shoulder.

His free hand clenched into a fist. No, he shouldn't have come. They could have said anything that needed saying in a terse phone call. He'd told himself that the entire time he was in the drugstore. At the hospital. But still he found himself making the drive out to the ranch, calling himself a fool with every passing mile.

"Why don't you sit down?" Cassie suggested.

"I won't be staying." He was far more comfortable keeping a distance between them. Even if he sat on a nearby chair, he'd be able to smell the shampoo in her hair, something fresh and lemony. He'd be able to see the softness of her skin, so at odds with the denim shirt and jeans. He'd remember all the times he'd stripped her and possessed every inch of that softness. Explored it by touch and sight and taste. The nights he'd lain awake with her in his arms, unwilling to sleep and miss a single moment of that magic.

And he'd remember anew the agony of their parting.

"Let's not do this again, Cass." His voice was raw. So were his feelings, though he'd half convinced himself he no longer possessed any. "Nothing's changed, and there's no reason to put ourselves through hell. It's over between us." The words burned his throat as he uttered them. But if they affected her, there was no sign of it on her face.

"You're right—it is over." She'd made the biggest mistake of her life when she'd trusted him with her secret. When she'd expected love to mean acceptance. It wasn't a mistake she'd repeat. And it had been an act of supreme self-indulgence. She knew what the future held for her. She'd dreamed it all too often in excruciating Technicolor detail. It would be hideously unfair to put a loved one through the pain caused by her death. It was better, far better, to limit the number of people it would impact.

She quieted the inner voice jeering at that thought and concentrated on the man before her. "I won't pretend I wasn't tempted to avoid this meeting. But you deserve to know the truth."

"The truth?" A corner of his mouth pulled downward. "I'm not sure you and I can ever agree on exactly what that means."

His words stung like tiny angry bees. "This has enough scientific evidence to satisfy even you. I'm pregnant. You're going to be a father."

Chapter 3

The news punched through him like a fist to the solar plexus, leeching his lungs of oxygen. Senses reeling, Shane shook his head a little, as if that would help him make sense of the incomprehensible.

"But…we were careful." As soon as he managed the words, he winced. As a doctor, he knew better than most the limitations of birth control. But shock was hazing his thinking, making logic difficult to summon. Cassie was pregnant. And the baby was his. He never entertained a doubt about that.

Raking her still slender form with his gaze, he demanded, "How far along?"

"Fourteen weeks."

"The bed-and-breakfast," he murmured.

"Probably."

For a moment their gazes caught, an unspoken sea of memories eddying between them. Sunlight slanting through the sheers at the window, long leisurely mornings spent in bed as the world had seemed to narrow its focus to just the two of them.

Before the memories could ensnare him, he neatly sidestepped them. "Who's your doctor? Have you had any tests yet? How's your health?" He cocked his head, his gaze turning professional. "How much weight have you gained? You are eating, aren't you?"

"Relax. I'm seeing Dr. Godden."

Satisfied, he gave a quick nod. "Joanne's good."

"And—" a corner of her mouth rose "—you should know by now that nothing could ever keep me from eating."

She managed to surprise a smile from him. "I remember. But nausea often accompanies the first few months of pregnancy. It'd be better if you could get through it on your own, but there are medications available if you can't."

"No nausea. I've gained two pounds already."

He frowned, crossed to sit next to her. "That's not enough."

"Dr. Godden isn't concerned. You shouldn't be either." She hesitated then, before adding briskly, "I mean that, too. I don't want you to worry about anything. Neither of us planned on this, but I'm going to keep the baby and raise it. I thought it would be easiest all around if I gave it my last name. You can be involved to whatever degree is comfortable for you, or not at all, if that's what you want. The decision is yours." The last few sentences came out in a rush, as if she'd practiced them long and hard and wanted them uttered before she lost her nerve.

She rose then, and turned toward the door. "I know this is a lot to lay on you all at once as soon

as you returned, so feel free to take your time thinking about it. You can let me know whatever you
decide.''

There was a little flare of anger directly beneath
his heart. As a dismissal, it wasn't particularly subtle.
Reaching for her hand, he tugged on it. She bounced
down on the couch again, and he kept her there, not
releasing his grip. He waited for her to look at him
before saying, ''A tidy little speech, Cass, designed
to let me off the hook. But you're overlooking one
thing—this baby is mine, too.'' Saying the words out
loud somehow made them feel more real. ''And I'd
never walk away. I intend to be fully involved.''
Abandonment came easily to some men. Certainly
his father had never looked back when he'd left over
twenty years ago. There was no way Shane would
ever do that to his own child. And the fact that Cassie
had thought he might hurt more than it should.

''I...'' Her gaze went to their hands. ''All right,
then. I just wanted you to know you had a choice.''

He smiled humorlessly. ''No. I don't.'' He didn't
expect her to know that, or to understand it. Emotional scars could last far longer than physical ones.
Every experience, especially the painful ones, left in-
delible marks on a person's character. And it wasn't
in Shane's to walk away from his responsibility, to
let his child grow up without a father in its life. He
hadn't changed that much.

''Okay, then.'' She tried for a smile, didn't quite
manage to pull it off. When she attempted to slip her
fingers from his grasp, he didn't let her. Wetting her
lips, she faced him squarely. ''I know this is com-
plicated, but it doesn't have to be. I'd never deny
you access to the child, and if you stay in the area,

there's no reason we can't share custody. I'd have some concerns with visitation, of course, if you decide to practice elsewhere, say out-of-state, at least until the child is older. But if—''

"I'm not going anywhere." Thirty minutes earlier he'd never have imagined uttering that sentence. He'd come back to Greenlaurel not knowing anymore who he was or where he belonged. But he had a piece of that answer now, from a most unexpected direction. He belonged with his child.

She tugged at her fingers again. "If you'd let me go, I'll get the ultrasound picture to show you."

He released her and she left the room, returning in a minute to hand him the picture. He'd seen many of them, of course. As a resident, he'd done a stint in the OB-GYN unit at Boston General.

So he was unprepared for the tide of emotion that ambushed him then, filling his chest and straining his heart. It shoved aside the clinical, scientific detachment he'd always examined these pictures with before. He stared at the white lines on the picture, detailing the tiny perfect form. Unconsciously he traced them with his forefinger. The baby had one small fist to its mouth, as if already searching for the contentment supplied by a miniature thumb. The date was stamped across the top, almost a month ago, with Cassie's name next to it.

"Shane?" Cassie's voice held a question. Only then did he realize how long he'd spent staring at the picture. "You can keep that if you want. I have another." When he didn't answer, couldn't, her voice grew uncertain. "Unless you've… Have you changed your mind?"

"No." Because his throat seemed full, he cleared

it. "I haven't changed my mind." The curtain of numbness that had shrouded his emotions for long months had begun shredding the moment he'd seen her letter, had rented when she'd opened the door and he'd seen her once again.

His defenses had crumbled when he'd taken one look at the tiny form in the picture and fully realized what it meant. *His child.*

He took one last glance at the picture before forcing himself to tuck it into his shirt pocket. "Did they tell you the sex?" Although the determination could be tricky at this early date, he had a good idea.

"I didn't ask."

He nodded, but his mind was already grappling with a host of other questions. Suddenly a decision that had seemed so easy only minutes ago became fraught with complication, although their situation was hardly an uncommon one. Children grew up all the time with split families.

He'd just never considered it for his child.

Dodging the bleakness that accompanied that thought, he said with more certainty than he was feeling, "We'll work it out. When's your due date?"

"April fourth."

"You should be cutting way back on your work around here." Concern flickered when he saw the mutinous look on her face. "Cass, you'll have to take things easy, especially this winter."

"Dr. Godden says I can continue doing what I'm doing as long as I feel up to it."

He opened his mouth to argue, then closed it again. Of course, that was standard medical advice for a woman with a low-risk pregnancy. But this was different. This was Cass. And the baby in question was his. It was oddly disconcerting to discover how easily science could be set aside when emotion was involved. He made a mental note to talk privately to Hawk about curtailing Cassie's activities around the ranch. Despite her slight stature, she worked as hard as any hand on the place. Common sense demanded that she exercise some restraint during the course of the pregnancy.

A sudden thought struck him. "Were you uncertain about the due date originally?"

He noticed the caution creeping into her eyes. "What do you mean?"

"Well, they usually don't order an ultrasound in the first trimester unless there's a reason for it. And you said your health is fine, so…"

"Yes, it was for the due date." It may have been his imagination but her response seemed rushed. "Like I told you, the baby is fine."

The phone rang then, and Cassie rose, not without a feeling of relief. She'd like to delay any discussion of the tests she'd undergone, and the reason for them, for as long as possible. Shane was very much a man of science. A discussion of her symptoms would only worry him, and he wouldn't put a lot of stock into the recipe for the tea Hawk had found for her.

As the phone sounded again, she quickened her step. Wild horses couldn't convince her to tell him about the brief flashes into the immediate future she'd been experiencing. She'd learned too late that he wasn't a man to accept anything that couldn't be proved and witnessed with his own eyes.

A moment after answering the phone she heard her brother's voice on the line and a delighted smile broke out. "You're not checking up on me, are you?

Because I can assure you, Jim makes a pretty effective watchdog.''

"Cassie, thank God.'' The urgency in his voice had the smile fading from her lips. "I've been trying to get in touch with you. I don't know how much time we have. You're in danger. Is Jim there? The other hands?'' She heard him swear, the impatience in his epithet familiar. "Damn. I suppose they've all gone home for the day.''

She frowned. "Hawk, what's wrong?'' A shiver raced down her spine, and the room seemed suddenly chilled.

"You need to get off the ranch. Now. Go to town and stay with...I don't know, any of your friends. Sheila maybe, if Rafe will be there. Just go somewhere safe and don't return until I get to town. It's going to take me a day or so. I haven't been able to get a flight yet. If I don't find something soon, I'll start driving.''

It was unusual to hear her taciturn brother string two sentences together at once. So this litany of terse orders didn't get her back up. It filled her with foreboding.

"You're going to have to be a bit more specific, Hawk. What's going on? What kind of danger are you talking about?'' She glanced up as Shane moved to her side. At his quizzical look, she shrugged. She couldn't tell him what was going on when she didn't understand herself.

Rather than snapping at her, as was his custom when she refused to fall in with his plans, he spoke faster. "Someone is coming for you. I don't know who will appear, but stay away from anyone you don't know, just to be safe. I can't give you details now. Just get out of there, Cassie, as quickly as possible.''

''There was a couple here about an hour ago,'' she said acerbically. ''They wanted to look at the horses we have listed on the sale bill. Irritating, certainly, but hardly cause for alarm.'' Annoyance had replaced trepidation. It wasn't like him to be so dramatic, but he'd been overprotective ever since he'd learned of her pregnancy, and the weird spells that had accompanied it.

''Who were they?'' His voice was sharp. ''What'd they look like?''

After Cassie described the strangers, she heard her brother's voice, sounding muffled, as though he were talking to someone next to him. ''Sheridan's found her. She's already been there.''

''Sheridan?'' The shiver was back, an electric current down her back. ''They introduced themselves as Billings.'' Even as she completed the sentence she knew the couple had lied. There had been something about them from the first that had made her wary. She'd explained away the feeling as a side effect of the mental flash she'd had that had preceded their arrival. Cassie swallowed around a throat that had gone suddenly dry. Aware of the man standing beside her, listening intently, she said, ''Hawk, I *knew* they were coming. Just like I knew about Baby.''

Her brother was silent as he digested the information. She'd called him on his cell a couple days ago, after she'd had one of those strange mental flashes. In this one she'd seen her brother's beloved dog, Baby, lying on the ground, blood pouring from its flank. Her brother hadn't been available to answer her call. But when they'd spoken later she'd learned her brother had been involved in a fight for his life, and his pet had been injured by a bullet meant for him.

"This is related to what you found out about our mother, isn't it? What haven't you told me about that? Why would people have tried to stop you from discovering the truth about her death?" She felt, rather than saw, Shane's reaction to her words.

"I'll tell you everything later," Hawk promised, a hint of desperation sounding in his voice. "But I think the woman who showed up at your door is Dr. Janet Sheridan. She's a chemist, and the man she works for will stop at nothing to get you, Cassie. She'll try to inject you with a drug they've designed. You can't let her near you."

The ground seemed to shift beneath her. There were, she thought numbly, more pieces than ever missing from the story her brother had yet to tell her about his adventures in the last few weeks. "Who is he?" she demanded. "How would he know about me?"

"That doesn't matter now. If the woman at your door was Sheridan, and from your description, it sure sounds like it, she's picked up some hired muscle to help her. I don't know why she left before kidnapping you, but you can't wait for her to come back."

"I know why." Cassie took a deep breath, forced herself to think rapidly. "Shane was coming up the drive. When they saw the car, they left, saying they'd be back tomorrow." After their initial insistence on seeing the horses, she'd thought it odd that they'd left in such a hurry. But when she'd discovered who was in the vehicle that had sent them on their way, all thoughts of the couple had abruptly faded.

"Farhold's there?" Hawk's voice was sharp. "Let me talk to him."

She hesitated, torn. Her brother had made no bones about his feelings about Shane when he and Cassie had broken up. But the decision was taken out of her hands, along with the phone.

Ignoring her glare, Shane took a few steps away, holding the cordless to his ear. "Hawk. What the hell's going on?"

"Get her out of there, Farhold. You've got to keep her safe. You owe her that much, at least."

The censure in the man's voice didn't come as a surprise. For all intents and purposes, he'd left Cassie alone and pregnant. Even if he had known about the baby, it wouldn't have changed what happened between the two of them. Couldn't change it even now.

"I heard most of what you told her on the phone," he said evenly. "And there was a car leaving as I came up the lane. You think the couple in it was after her? But why?"

"I'm as certain as I can be. So is the FBI. They're involved in this case, too. I don't have time to go into it. Just get her to town and watch her every second. I'll get there as soon as I can, and the Bureau is sending agents, as well. The danger is real, Shane. Make her believe it. And keep her safe. This guy who's after her, he's—" The line went abruptly dead.

"Hawk?" When there was no answer, he clicked off the phone and looked at Cassie. "His phone must have gone dead. Was he calling from his cell?"

"Check the caller ID." He pressed the button on the receiver that should have displayed the numbers of incoming calls. The screen remained blank.

"Looks like it was your phone that went dead."

She went to the den and retrieved her cell phone from its cradle. As she reentered the living room, she flicked on the light switch, then stopped midstride when the light failed to go on. She swallowed hard, caught his gaze on her. "The electricity is off."

A grim mask slid over his expression. "Any chance it happened earlier today and you just didn't notice?"

She thought for a moment. "I used the microwave and the stove about three hours before you got here. It could have gone off anytime since then, I suppose."

He went to the window, peered out into the rapidly descending dusk. "There's no sign of anyone out front. Any other way to get to the ranch without using the lane?"

"Not unless someone got to the main road and cut the fence, came up a quarter mile or so from here and circled around back." The likelihood of that scenario was remote. But then, the whole scene Hawk had warned her of had a vaguely surreal aspect to it.

"Grab a bag and throw a few things together," Shane said. "You're staying with me until we get this figured out." As he spoke he moved to the door, locked it. She stared at him, swaying a bit on her feet as his figure moved into and out of focus. His words seemed to come from a distance and there was an all too familiar sense of velocity, as though she was being catapulted through space. Her pulse galloped as her vision dimmed, rainbows arrayed beneath her eyelids. The cell phone slipped from her hand, clattered unnoticed to the floor. And then it was as if a giant curtain was slung aside, bits of mental images whirling and colliding before forming yet another scene.

Shane was striding across the room in front of the window. There was the sound of a shot, and the glass shattered, spraying across the room.

''Cass!''

She blinked rapidly, noting the insistence in the word, if not the meaning. Her vision cleared, leaving her feeling weak and limp. She was seated, although she didn't remember sitting down, and Shane was kneeling in front of her, his hands over hers, his face concerned.

''Are you all right?''

''Fine.'' She tried to summon a smile, doubted she pulled it off. Rising, she prayed her knees would hold her. ''I'll get a bag. You'll need to lock the other two doors.''

Shane got to his feet, still watching her strangely. ''I already did.''

Although she had no memory of it at all, she nodded. ''I'll just be a minute.'' She took several steps before hesitating, flashes of that last mental image appearing again in her mind. ''Come with me.''

He did, driven out of an anxiety he didn't voice. She was still white, still shaky, and he didn't trust her to not collapse before making it to her room. But she moved at record speed, dragging a small bag out of her closet and throwing in a change of clothes, then crossing to the adjoining bath to pack some toiletries. He went to the window in her room and looked out, the lengthening shadows making it difficult to see anything. It'd be fully dark in another fifteen minutes. Night never used to hold any particular fears for him. Not until he discovered firsthand how many black-hearted thieves and murderers prowled beneath its mantle. The knowledge was enough to keep his instincts razor sharp.

He looked up as Cassie reentered the room, noted that she'd regained a bit of color. "Let's go," he said, taking her elbow and leading her out the door. "We can contact Hawk again once we get to town."

"I could call him now from my cell."

"It's going to take someone with a better hand at electronics than me to put your cell phone back together, if it can be salvaged at all." At her blank look, he added, "You dropped it. Remember?"

But when she got to the living room and saw the pieces of what had been her phone heaped on the end table, she bit her lip. The truth was, she didn't remember. Not the moments leading up to the vision, not those immediately following it.

A feeling of unease stabbed through her. The episodes had never before occurred so closely together. She needed to get the ingredients for the tea from the kitchen and pack it for her trip to town. In addition to their increasing frequency, the experiences were also getting stronger.

She was crossing to the kitchen when something made her turn. Her blood froze as she saw Shane close the curtain beside one window, approach the next to do the same thing.

"Stay away from the window!"

Her voice was sharp as she started toward him. He turned his head, frowned, but never broke his stride. "Get the rest of your things, Cass. I'll feel better once I have you back in town."

His words were lost on her. Racing across the room, she dove at him, hitting him square in the back and knocking him to the floor. As if on cue, the window above them exploded, tiny shards of glass raining down on them as they lay, panting for breath, on the floor.

She'd landed on top of him when she fell, but the impact had driven the air from her lungs. As she hauled in oxygen, she heard him mutter, "What the hell? Are you all right?"

"Someone…shot at you." Gulping for air, she raised her head and pointed. He followed the direction with his gaze, stilled when he saw the splintered hole in the side of the entertainment center, which had been directly to his left.

"You saw someone out there?" He grasped her elbows, raised her to her feet, none too gently. "And you still raced over here putting yourself in line of the bullet?" He gave her a shake, his face harsh. "You try something like that again, and pregnant or not, I'll paddle your ass."

Her lungs had returned to normal, as had her temper. "You could try, anyway." Yanking herself from his grasp, she moved cautiously until she was out of the line of vision from any of the windows. Only then did she rise. When she did, she found Shane right beside her. She didn't remember him being able to move that fast before. Or that silently.

"You don't want to push me, Cass." There was a thread of meanness to his voice that was as unfamiliar as the bleakness in his eyes. "I'm not the same man you knew a few months ago."

Her stomach hollowed out, and the danger surrounding them abruptly receded in the face of the truth in his words. She'd already recognized that, hadn't she, the moment she'd opened the door and seen him again? There was a far more subtle difference than the scar tracing down his throat. And whatever had caused the difference, she was achingly aware he'd suffered profoundly for it. "Who are you, then?" she whispered, not expecting an answer.

He stared at her for a long moment, before stepping back and turning away. His voice sounded raw when he responded. "Damned if I know."

Struggling to make sense of his words, she watched as he went to the gun cabinet on the wall. Her jaw dropped open as he opened it and took out a rifle. The sight of Dr. Shane Farhold with a gun in his hands, and, she recognized incredulously, handling it with some degree of familiarity, was incomprehensible. He'd never made any secret of his disapproval of gun ownership. He'd lost too many gunshot wound victims on the operating table, he'd once told her, to have any respect for gun advocates' argument promoting the so-called right to bear arms. She'd understood the source of his distaste, even if she hadn't agreed with it.

So it was doubly shocking to see him hefting the rifle to his shoulder, sighting it, before lowering it to ask, "Where do you keep the ammunition?"

It took a couple attempts before she could manage an answer. "Top shelf, hallway closet." As he strode off, she carefully made her way to the wall, wincing as shards of glass crunched beneath her feet. Sidling along the wall to the window, she reached out, pulled the curtain.

A beam of light appeared, as Shane approached her again. "I found flashlights up there, too."

"Hawk believes in being prepared." And so did she. Without a word, she reached out, took the flash-

light from him and went to the gun case. If her
brother was right, there were two people outside
waiting for them. With both her and Shane armed,
the odds evened.

"I don't get it. According to Hawk, the couple
who was here earlier has orders to kidnap me." The
words sounded even more ludicrous for being spoken
out loud. "So why would they be shooting?"

"The shot wasn't meant for you. If your brother
is right, they'll want you alive. Right now I'm the
only person standing between you and them." His
voice was matter of fact in the near darkness. "By
eliminating me, they'll be a heck of a lot closer to
their goal."

"Like hell," Cassie muttered. She had no idea
what Hawk was involved in, or how it affected her.
But she knew intuitively that if the couple outside
ever succeeded in their mission, she'd never return
to the ranch alive.

Memory flickered, of the dream that had haunted
her all her life. The stranger on her doorstep wasn't
the murderer from her nightmares. The two men had
different coloring and physical builds. But that didn't
mean that her kidnapping wouldn't start a sequence
of events that would result in the final enactment of
the dream.

She may have to accept the finality of her own
end, but she'd never accept that for her unborn child.

"Shine that light over here so I can load."

Obediently, she swung the beam of light toward
the direction of Shane's voice. Although his movements weren't as rapid and automatic as her own
would be, there was no doubt he'd done this before.

When he'd finished, without a word she took his gun and handed him hers to load.

"What about your cell? If we called the sheriff, he could be out here in twenty minutes."

Shane's mouth flattened. "I didn't bring it." There was a sound then that had them both going silent, straining to listen.

Someone was on the front porch.

Cassie's gaze went to the door handle, watched it twist slowly, first one way, then the other. Setting the flashlight down, she reached for her gun.

Shane grabbed his as well, and as if one, they walked silently to the kitchen, to the side door that led into the mudroom. They waited for long tension-filled moments, before hearing the sound of that door being tried.

Then swiftly, Shane brought the rifle to his shoulder, aimed and fired through the curtained window beside the door. They heard a muttered curse, footsteps running down the steps.

Cassie couldn't prevent a tiny grin. "Sounds like you gave them something to think about."

"For now, at least." Shane crossed to her side and they went back to the kitchen. "But they've got all night, and we can't be positive it's just the two of them. We can't watch all four sides of the house indefinitely." If the couple out there wanted in badly enough, he was afraid they just might succeed. There were any number of windows that would provide access. And there was the outside chance that, if pressed, they'd try something even more daring.

"We could make a run for your car. With each of us providing cover for the other, we could probably make it, especially now that it's dark."

"They've probably already made sure the car is useless to us." It was what he would do. Slit the tires or remove a distributor cap. "And if we leave here for a vehicle that's been taken out of commission, we just put ourselves at their mercy."

"Okay. We can probably hold them off until daylight. Jim and the other hands are usually here by six-thirty. That's only nine hours or so."

He knew they didn't have that long. He looked at her, barely able to make out her features in the darkness. "If they're as desperate as Hawk seemed to believe, they're going to find a way in before then. We need to think of something else."

She was silent long enough to have him watching her closely. The urgency of their situation would be enough to send most women into hysterics, and Cassie had looked on the verge of collapse just a few minutes earlier. But her voice, when she finally spoke, sounded remarkably steady.

"All right, then. I think our best chance is to make a run for it."

Chapter 4

"What are you planning?" Shane couldn't suppress a flicker of admiration. Not many women would be able to calmly map out escape routes with at least two armed intruders right outside. But in contrast to her earlier shaky moments, Cassie was composed.

"When we were kids, Hawk and I used to sneak out when the moon was full, to go for rides while our parents were sleeping. I think I can get us to the barn undetected."

Shane considered the idea. "Are the pickups in there?" It was doubtful the couple outside hadn't already rendered them undrivable, but it was worth a shot.

"Jim has one. The other should be parked nearby. It probably has been tampered with," she added, as if reading his thoughts. "I think our best way out of here is by horseback."

He was already shaking his head. "There's no way

we could get all the way back to town without having to take the road, eventually. We'd be walking right into their arms.''

"I'm not trying to get us to town. I'm thinking of heading for the forest.''

He started to dismiss the idea, before realizing it had merit. If they could get a good head start, or, better yet, give the kidnappers the slip completely, they could vanish into the wilderness, and to safety.

The plan wasn't without risk, however. With the full moon, visibility would be better than usual. If they were spotted, they'd be sitting ducks. And the horses couldn't outpace a vehicle, at least until they got to rougher terrain. He had no idea how many miles of open country they had to pass through to get to the forest bordering the area.

"There's a cabin in the forest that my family used to camp in. We can hide there.'' She paused, but when he still said nothing, a hint of impatience crept into her tone. "Well? What do you think?''

He was thinking that the risks were unacceptable. There was no way in hell he was willing to thrust Cassie and the baby into that kind of danger. But the situation was perilous, regardless. And he'd learned in Afghanistan that sometimes decisions had to be made when neither choice was entirely acceptable.

Hopefully, living with the consequences of this choice would prove easier than the one he'd made there.

"Let's do it.'' With the words came a sense of, if not peace, at least resolution. There were few in the state who could match Cassie's riding ability, and she was familiar with the forest in a way the kidnappers couldn't be. If something happened to him, she'd still have a good chance of getting away on her own. And those were probably the best odds they were going to get in this situation.

"You'll need to pack, too." Her voice was brisk. "You can use Hawk's things. You're close enough to the same size. There's a backpack in his closet. Make sure you wear a pair of his boots. I'll get some blankets and food, and a heavier coat for you."

"Call for me if you hear anything. I mean *anything,* Cass."

She nodded, gave him a nudge to get him moving. "I will. Promise." Only then did he turn and stride toward the bedrooms. She went to the kitchen and quickly found two thermoses to fill. Then she emptied the refrigerator of anything that could be eaten easily and wouldn't spoil. A foot-long summer sausage and deer sticks. Oranges, bananas and apples. She piled items on the counter, withstanding the temptation to take more. It wouldn't take Hawk long to get here, and the lighter their load, the faster the horses could travel.

She grabbed her bag and went back to her room. Entering cautiously, she crawled along the floor to stay out of sight of the windows, until she could yank the curtains closed. Then she retrieved her bag, dumping its contents in the middle of the bed. Swiftly she repacked, this time stuffing warm clothes into a backpack from her closet. She changed, pulling on a heavy sweater, thick socks and scuffed boots. The linen closet was raided for blankets, and she made two crude bedrolls, securing them with ponytail holders. Satisfied, she took her pack into the kitchen, and put the food she'd gathered into it.

"I found some more stuff in the hallway closet."

Cassie started a little at the sound of Shane's voice. Turning, she found him standing in the doorway. "I packed a couple flashlights, extra batteries, compass and more ammo. Did you think of blankets?"

"They're ready to go, on my floor." While he went to get them, she went to the mudroom, shrugged into a coat. Grabbing one for Shane, she headed back out to meet him. Her step faltered as she noticed that he had stilled, his head cocked, listening. She stopped. "What is it?" she whispered. But then she heard the noise that had captured his attention and her flesh prickled.

Someone was on the roof.

Icy fingers of fear traced down her spine. There was no way into the attic from the roof. But knowing that didn't dispel the chill. From that vantage point the intruder would have an excellent view of the grounds. If he, or she, happened to be looking in the right direction at just the right time...Cassie shuddered.

"It's a good time to move." Shane's voice was even. "There may only be one on the ground now. How are we getting out of the house?"

She handed him the coat she'd found for him. "The root cellar." Her pulse was hammering, adrenaline surging through her veins. "They may have already tried the door, but it's well secured from the inside."

"We need a distraction. Something to draw their attention for a few minutes to the other side of the house." Shane thought rapidly, examining options, discarding them. "Once we take these things downstairs, I'll come back up and break a window, make some noise. Hopefully that'll draw them both away long enough for us to get to the barn unnoticed. Here.'' He handed her a flashlight, then lifted their packs and the guns, leaving a bedroll for Cassie to carry. Then he followed her to the mudroom. She opened a door he'd never paid much attention to before and he followed the beam of light down the steep steps.

The area wasn't much more than the cellar she'd called it. Limestone walls lined the space, and the clammy dampness immediately seemed to close in on them. He followed her to an old oversize wooden door. Then he stepped in front of her, slipping his load to the cement floor, and keeping his rifle ready. Motioning her back, he listened intently, but heard nothing. Bringing the rifle to his shoulder, he unfastened the bolt and opened the door.

The flashlight beam showed nothing more sinister than cobwebs on the stone steps that led up to the outside door. He climbed the stairs, examined the door. It didn't look as though it had been tampered with, and the lock was still secured. Satisfied, he reclosed the door and retraced his steps back to Cassie.

''Okay. When you hear me coming back down the stairs, get the door open and be ready to move.''

She nodded, and he hesitated, strangely torn about leaving her, even for a few moments. For a moment he had second thoughts about the plan. During their run from the house to the barn they'd be completely vulnerable. If discovered along the way, there was nothing more substantial than the corral fence to provide cover. But try as he might, he couldn't think of a better idea.

''There's a cast-iron statue of a dog next to the

fireplace in the living room. You can use that to break the window.''

Cassie's suggestion interrupted his thoughts. And because his doubts served no useful purpose, he shoved them aside. The plan would work because it had to. Survival, he'd discovered, was a pretty powerful motivator. "Wait until you hear me come down the steps," he reminded her. Without waiting to see her nod, he grabbed the rifle and slipped back up the stairs.

Once he got back into the kitchen he could hear the sounds on the roof again. Swiftly he crossed to the other room to retrieve the statue Cassie had mentioned, then stopped short before he was halfway across the space.

There was an odd hissing sound nearby, and Shane craned his neck, trying to pinpoint the noise. The electricity was still off, so it couldn't be the furnace or an appliance. Scanning the darkness, he moved slowly through the room, discovering that it grew louder the closer he drew to the fireplace.

The fireplace.

Twin observations occurred simultaneously. The foreign aroma, slightly sweet, and the sound he'd heard could only mean one thing. The person on the roof had tossed something down the chimney.

Eyes already tearing, Shane backpedaled rapidly. He raced to the kitchen, grabbed the cast-iron skillet off the top of the stove. He rifled through drawers until he found a kitchen towel, and used it to cover his mouth and nose. Then he ran to the front of the house and heaved the skillet through the upper portion of one window.

Glass broke with a satisfying crash, before the skillet landed with a thud on the porch floor outside. Shane turned to make his way back to the kitchen, found himself moving drunkenly. He shook his head to clear it. Dots were hazing his vision, and it took longer than it should have to find his way back to his rifle, and then to the basement door.

As soon as Cassie heard him at the top of the steps, she unfastened the bolt on the door and went back to their packs, expecting to find Shane ready to move. But she was surprised to discover he hadn't even made it down the stairs yet.

Instincts immediately heightened, she bolted toward him, just as he started down. Halfway down he stumbled, practically falling the rest of the way. She reached out to him. "What's wrong?"

"Something down the chimney." His words were a bit slurred and difficult to make out. "Gotta get out." Because he was swaying just a bit, she slipped her arm around his waist and helped him across the small area to where their bags were heaped, waiting for them.

"I can get most of this stuff." Cassie was more worried than she wanted to admit. Was the strange substance he'd inhaled dangerous? What if he suffered long-term ill effects? But Shane was still feeling sufficiently well to prevent her from carrying too much. He slipped the backpacks over one arm, leaving one hand free for his rifle. Cassie scooped up the two bedrolls and tucked them under her arm before snatching up the extra gun. She watched his form carefully as he headed up the stairs to the outside door in front of her. Other than a slight wobble, he appeared to be already recovering.

The door was eased open. Cassie held her breath

as they both paused for a moment. Then Shane whispered, "Okay. Stay low and run like hell. I'll cover you."

"It'd be better if you go first and I cover you," she argued in a low voice. He was the one the kidnappers would find dispensable. If they wanted her alive, it was unlikely they'd shoot at her. And although it wasn't the ideal time for a debate on the issue, he couldn't fault her reasoning.

He didn't try. He just nudged her out the door urgently and ordered, "Move!"

The time for arguing was over. Even a few steps out into the night air, she already felt exposed and vulnerable. She ran. The full moon overhead felt like a spotlight. If the intruders were anywhere on this side of the house... If Shane had failed to distract them... If the one on the roof happened to look this way...

Cassie stifled the doubts creeping into her mind like busy little ants and concentrated on stepping lightly and staying crouched. Sending a sidelong glance at Shane, she found him with his rifle ready, his gaze sweeping the area as he ran beside her.

It was probably only sixty yards to the barn, but the distance seemed interminable. Cassie couldn't see anyone in the vicinity, but she also couldn't make out any strange vehicles, and she knew there had to be at least one nearby. After a moment she just gave up trying to peer through the shadows and concentrated on reaching the barn in record time.

The building didn't seem to be getting any closer. She felt as though she was running in slow motion, although her legs already ached and her lungs were heaving. At any moment she expected to hear the sound of a shot ringing out, voices shouting, something to signify that they'd been discovered. But there was nothing, other than the sound of Shane's breathing and her own. The silence was eerie.

Finally the barn loomed before her. With a sigh of relief, she burst inside, feeling Shane on her heels. Knees suddenly weak, she slowed, and then stopped. "I'm going to stay here and watch," he said, the words nearly soundless. "You get the horses ready."

She didn't move. "Are you all right?" He'd been visibly affected by whatever the kidnapper had put down the chimney while in the basement.

"I'm fine." It was his voice that convinced her. Stronger now, it lacked the slurring that had marred it earlier. "The fresh air cleared my head, and I had my face covered part of the time upstairs."

"What do you think it was?"

She felt, rather than saw, his shrug. "Some type of gas, I imagine. Nothing too lethal, or they would have risked you, too. From the way it affected me, it was probably designed to make us groggy, or knock us out completely."

Relieved that he seemed recovered, she wasted no more time on words, turning toward the horses. The confines of the barn were shadowy, the moonlight slanting through the entrances on opposite sides of the interior. Stalls lined one wall, though most of them were empty. The majority of the stock was pastured. The only horses being kept in the barn right now were those targeted for sale.

She made her selections rapidly. The large roan had a smooth gait and loved to run. It whickered a little as she saddled it, swishing its tail and sidestepping until Cassie murmured to it soothingly, calming it. She tied one bedroll behind the saddle, then slipped out of the stall.

Turning, she saw Shane just inside the doorway, facing the direction of the house. The sight had her quickening her step. If he was right and the intruders had hoped to knock them out, it followed that their next move would be to enter the house, expecting to find them both out of commission. Once inside, it wouldn't take them long to discover that it was empty.

She chose a high-spirited midsized sorrel for herself. Once she'd readied it, she rattled a feed bucket a little, attracting Shane's attention, and motioned him over.

He approached swiftly. She took the remaining bedroll and her bag, securing it to her horse. "Yours is ready to go, too. Three stalls down." While Shane went after the roan, she reached for one of the guns he'd leaned against the wall of the corridor, and slipped it in the rifle scabbard. When he led his horse to her, she fastened the backpack on it, secured the rifle and gave a satisfied nod.

Leaving her to follow with the horses, Shane headed for the entrance at the opposite side of the barn. When she reached him, he waved at her to wait and slipped outside to run the length of the barn and check the area.

While she waited, Cassie mounted, holding the reins of the roan until he'd returned. "I don't see anything," he said, mounting and taking the reins from her.

"Then we'll ride out fast, heading east. Wherever they've stashed their vehicle, it can't be far. The fences will slow them down a bit." She stopped at that, looked at him. "How comfortable are you with jumping?" They'd ridden together many times, but she was far more familiar with horses than he, having grown up around them.

He gave her a humorless smile. "I'm more comfortable with jumping than I am with being shot at."

She shuddered, failing to take any amusement from the remark. "Stay low in the saddle so you don't give them a target." There was no way the kidnappers could avoid hearing the horses as they galloped away, which meant it was all the more imperative that they quickly put as much distance between themselves and the intruders as possible.

But before she could put that thought into action, a voice behind them sounded. "You make a damn good target right now, and I'm a hell of a shot."

Cassie jerked around in the saddle. The first thing she focused on was the automatic weapon pointed at them. The next was the man holding it. The same man who had been on her porch earlier that day.

Stan, or whatever his real name was, gestured at her with the gun. "Slide down off that horse, lady. But first, both of you take out those rifles nice and slow and drop them to the ground."

Every organ in her body seemed encased in ice. Even frozen as she was, however, she was aware of Shane. He was moving his horse closer. She knew intuitively he'd try to place himself between her and the gunman. Deliberately she tightened her grip on the left rein, forcing her horse to dance to the side, thwarting his attempt.

"Maybe you don't think I'm serious." Menace crept into the man's tone, and his finger tightened over the trigger. "Don't think about being a hero, buddy. She's too close for me to miss and I will shoot her first.''

"No, you won't." Shane sounded amazingly calm. "Your boss ordered you to bring her in alive, didn't he? She wouldn't be much use to him dead."

There was a flicker of surprise on the man's face, although he recovered swiftly. "She can survive a bullet through the knee, though, can't she?" He raised a transmitter to his mouth and spoke into it. "I've got them. Yeah, far side of the barn. They went for the horses." Then he lowered it, took a step closer to Cassie. "How about you, lady? Do you care if I put a bullet through your friend's brain? I don't need him alive."

"Yes." She drew a long breath, and the quaver in her voice wasn't difficult to summon. "Please, don't hurt him. I'll do anything you ask."

"Cassie, no!"

Ignoring Shane's sharp cry, she drew the rifle slowly from the scabbard, inching the horse closer to the man as she babbled. "I'll go with you. Just promise you won't hurt him. He won't tell anyone, please."

"Shut up and drop the rifle. You, too, buddy."

"I'm putting it down, see?" She began to lower the gun, edged nearer. "Just promise you'll let him go."

"Dammit, Cassie—"

She barely heard Shane's words because at that moment she yanked on the reins, heeled her horse hard. The sorrel reared, one flailing hoof catching the man in the shoulder. He stumbled back, dropping his gun. She had the horse rear again, and the man did a mad scramble backward on the ground, frantic to distance himself from the sharp hooves. Only then did she wheel the horse around, heel it sharply, urging it to run. "Go!" she yelled at Shane as her horse leaped past him.

His roan raced along with hers, galloping past the paddocks and training corrals. Casting a quick glance his way, she saw he was keeping his form low over the horse's neck, as she was. A moment later there was a sharp crack as a bullet whizzed by them. And then another. The third was close enough to kick up the dirt between their horses. She could hear voices shouting behind them, but didn't dare turn around. The wind was in her face, brisk with fall chill. Her hair was whipping behind her; she'd forgotten to secure it. And every instinct she had was screaming at her that the next bullet could end everything.

But there were no more bullets. Whatever the reason, the shooting had stopped for the moment. She cut across the pastures, hoping fence line would slow the couple's pursuit. She never doubted they'd come after them. She just hoped they had enough of a head start.

"Remind me to punish you for that little stunt later," Shane called over, his voice grim.

A giddy sense of elation filled her. "It seemed like a good idea at the time." She felt the horse tense beneath her before she noticed the barbed wire looming before them. The sorrel cleared it effortlessly, barely breaking stride. She heard the roan land behind her. Riding horses across the fields at night wasn't a good idea in the best of conditions. The mount could step in a gopher hole and break a leg, or it could shy in the face of one of the night predators out searching for prey, throwing the rider. Having the horses jumping fence was an even worse idea.

But the danger behind them somehow minimized the risks they were taking right now.

"How far to the timberline?" Shane called.

"I'm not sure. Ten, fifteen miles." They rode in silence then, urgency palpable between them. Several times she looked over her shoulder, half-expecting to see the man who'd accosted them right on their heels. But there was only moonlight-dappled fields, other horses watching them quizzically, the sound of hooves thundering as they kept up a swift pace.

Their mounts took the next fence as if they'd been bred to do so. Cassie experienced a moment of euphoria as they leaped through the air, despite the desperation of their situation. They were going to do it. Certainty mixed with adrenaline. They were going to get away completely. She allowed herself a tiny smile, but something compelled her to turn and look, one more time.

Her smile abruptly faded. There in the distance, far behind but unmistakable, was the glare of headlights. She looked at Shane. "They're coming."

"I know." He sent her a reassuring glance. "We've got a good head start, though."

She swallowed hard, faced ahead. They had a good five minutes on the kidnappers, and the route she'd picked would make it difficult for any vehicle to follow at full speed without damaging an axle. The fences, too, would slow them down.

But none of those things would stop them. Cassie was sure of that. And their horses wouldn't be able to keep up this pace indefinitely.

They rode several more minutes before Cassie

chanced a look behind them again. To her dismay, the headlights were a great deal closer. If the couple was still driving the four-wheel-drive pickup they'd had earlier, their trek across the pastures would be easier.

Making a sudden decision, she shouted, "Veer right." Shane obeyed. They took another fence and galloped toward a small stream that meandered across the ranch. Already the terrain was changing, growing rockier and rougher. She could only hope it would hinder their pursuers. The sorrel was tiring, and she didn't try to urge it faster. The timberline was up ahead, and the ground sloped steadily upward. Both horses slowed to a canter.

Pines dotted the area, interspersed with mesquite and sweet gums. The vegetation would eventually grow denser with oaks, elms, junipers and pecans, making it impossible to follow in a vehicle. But first they had to reach the forest.

"Only another couple miles," she told Shane, and he nodded. Neither mentioned what they'd both noticed—that the truck had drawn a bit closer than before. Instead, they guided their horses around thickets of mesquite and clumps of pine, trying to choose a path that would be more difficult to follow. There was no way to reduce their visibility, not with the full moon spotlighting them.

Cassie estimated the distance before they reached the forest entrance, and relative safety. Another ten minutes at this pace should do it. Once safely engulfed in its interior, she'd need to consult the compass to get her bearings. They'd be approaching the cabin from a different direction than the one she usually took. The last thing she wanted was to lead Shane in circles.

A small animal darted out of a clump of mesquite then, directly across her path. The sorrel startled, danced sideways nervously, then stumbled. Cassie fought to remain in her seat. "Easy, boy, take it easy now," she said soothingly. But when the horse straightened again and moved forward, there was a noticeable limp to its gait.

"Are you okay?"

The concern in Shane's voice registered, even as she was slipping off the horse. Kneeling at its side, she ran her fingers along its right front leg. There was already swelling apparent on the cannon. After a bit further examination, relief mingled with dismay. The leg didn't appear broken.

"I'm fine," she told Shane belatedly. "But the horse has a sprain. I'll have to turn it back and ride the rest of the way with you."

"Let's do it."

She handed him her backpack to secure next to his while she unfastened their bedrolls. Using the saddle strings, she tied them to the D-rings on either side of the saddle. Turning back to her sorrel, she looped the reins securely around the saddle horn, before stroking a hand down her horse's neck. "Go home, big guy. Get on now." Backing up, she gave it a slap on its rump, and it started picking its way slowly back down the slope.

Shane extended a hand and Cassie took it as she put her foot in the stirrup and swung up on the back of his horse. Only then did she cast a glance at the lights moving inexorably toward them. "Don't worry," Shane said, as if reading her thoughts.

"They'll have to abandon their vehicle before we do the horse. We still have a lead."

"I know." But she also knew that the kidnappers were armed. And if they drew any closer before she and Shane could disappear into the forest, they'd be within shooting range. Maybe it was just as well she had to ride behind Shane, despite the slower pace. She effectively blocked him as a target. If Hawk had been right about their pursuers' purpose, they wouldn't chance shooting her in an attempt to hit Shane.

She'd have to take what solace she could from that.

"I ought to kill you right here." The gun felt natural in Janet Sheridan's hand, and it was taking every ounce of self-control she possessed to keep from putting a bullet in the man's small brain. A steady fog of rage rose, hazing intellect. Failure was unacceptable. *Unacceptable.* She'd never failed at anything in her life, and the possibility of it now, because of this cretin's ineptitude, was feeding a ravenous fury. "We should have taken the woman at the ranch this afternoon."

"Someone was coming." Jack Nearling's voice was sullen, but wary. He must realize how close to death he was right now, which meant he had a modicum of intelligence. "You're the one who said to do it without witnesses. Why else did we wait for the hands to leave for the day?"

Was he actually blaming this fiasco on *her?* Janet's finger squeezed the trigger a fraction, thinking of how satisfying it would be to splatter the man's brains against the window. "You had them in your

sights, you idiotic fool. All you had to do was shoot
the man, and we'd have had her. Only an imbecile
could screw that up.''

- Jack's jaw went tight, and he slid a sidelong glance
at the gun, before training his gaze on the rocky terrain ahead. ''They were armed, and they both jumped
me at once. What was I supposed to do? I still managed to get a couple shots off, didn't I?''

She smiled, a humorless stretching of lips over
teeth. ''You can't shoot any better than you can follow orders. Had you waited for me to get there we
wouldn't be in this mess.'' Just the thought of Benedict's reaction to this problem sent a cold sheet of
sweat creeping across her brow. Her boss and some-
time lover, Benedict Payne didn't tolerate failure.
Just the thought of calling him about this disaster had
her mouth going dry. She might as well turn the gun
on herself, because her life wouldn't be worth a dime
if she disappointed him.

''Listen, you're acting like it's over and it's not.''
A thread of worry had crept into Jack's voice. Janet
barely noticed it. How would Benedict arrange her
own end? she wondered sickly. Would he dispatch
one of his men to take her out when she was least
expecting it? Or would he do it himself, choking the
life out of her as she'd once seen him do to a chemist
who had threatened disloyalty? There was a boulder-
sized knot in her throat and she couldn't seem to
breathe. She could wonder about her death, but she
couldn't doubt it. Benedict didn't tolerate failure any
more than she did.

''They're heading for the forest, we know that.''
Slowly, the man's voice registered. ''They think
they'll be safe there, but they aren't. We'll just go in

after them. I'm a pretty fair tracker. Learned it from my dad. It's pretty damn hard to move through the wilderness without leaving a trace."

She watched him emotionlessly. Chances were, he was lying, trying to save his miserable life.

"C'mon." The truck jolted over an unseen rock, shuddered, then stalled. "I grew up in eastern Texas. Been in and around forest all my life. I can find them. If they take the horse into the wilderness, they'll have to stick to some sort of trail. If they go in on foot, I can still track them."

Janet released the pressure on the trigger and considered. The man was desperate, that was evident. Desperation led to all sorts of exaggeration. But if there was even the slightest chance that he could do as he said, she could afford to spare his life. For now.

"Let's hope you're even half as good as you claim." She slipped the safety back on and lowered the gun. "Because if you fail again, I won't use a bullet on you. That's too easy." She thought of the syringes in her pack and smiled unpleasantly. "I have something far worse in mind."

She could read the relief on the man's face and nearly laughed. She didn't suffer fools easily and once he'd outlived his usefulness, he'd die, just as the one before him had. But first she'd see if he could lead them to Donovan. Once she got rid of the woman's companion and had her safely injected, she'd take care of the man at her side. Resolve replaced the cold terror she'd felt earlier. Nothing would stop her from taking the woman back to Benedict. Each of them had his or her own unique fate.

And she was going to be the one to make sure that Cassie Donovan met hers.

Chapter 5

Shane and Cassie plunged into the forest as if the hounds of hell were snapping at their heels. It was, Shane mused grimly, an apt analogy. The darkness of the interior swallowed them up, in marked contrast to the bright moonlight outside. He handed Cassie one of the flashlights, retaining the other. They clicked them on simultaneously.

"I'll need to use the compass to navigate the way to the cabin." Cassie's whisper sounded out of place in the quiet.

"Is it in your pack or mine?" he asked, sweeping the area with the beam of the flashlight. The forest floor locked like a tangle of underbrush, and for the first time he considered the trail they would undoubtedly leave. It couldn't be helped, however. At least the darkness would make it difficult to follow them.

"Mine." She turned so he could unzip the pack she had on her back and rummaged inside it until he found the compass. He handed it to her, and she held it under the beam of her light, expression intent.

He used the time to study her. If she was fatigued by their adventure, it didn't show in her face. She had her bottom lip caught between her teeth, the way she always did when she was concentrating on something. His gaze lingered there, remembering all too clearly the softness of her lips, their fullness, the taste of them that had never failed to strip his mind clean.

It had been his unprecedented reaction to her that had allowed her to get so close to him so fast. He had a lifetime of experience keeping his defenses raised. But there had been something about her from the first time he'd seen her. He'd attended an excruciatingly dull hospital benefit, had been counting the minutes until he could steal away…and then he'd caught sight of her standing across the room, talking to his friend Simon. It had been her looks that had drawn him across the floor, the sound of her laugh that had kept him waiting, impatiently, for Simon to introduce them.

And once he'd gotten close enough to see that hint of sadness in those amazing grass green eyes of hers, he'd been caught. Neatly and irrevocably. He couldn't have walked away even if he'd wanted to. And it had been months before he'd wanted to.

The memories had sharp edges. Deliberately, he looked away. "Are you ready?" His voice was more brusque than he'd meant it to be.

"Yep." She shoved the compass into her coat pocket and began walking. "The cabin is northeast of here. I don't even want to guess how long a walk it is, though. We're pretty wide of the way I usually go."

"Just as well." He fell in behind her. "We need to steer clear of any well-traveled paths." Not that he could see anything resembling a path ahead of them. The vines covering the forest floor almost seemed alive, swirling on the ground and clutching at his ankles with every step he took. "It'll be slower going through the thickest part of the forest, but it'll be just as hard for anyone coming after us. We want to move as fast as we can, while leaving as little trail as possible."

Cassie looked over her shoulder at him. "You think they'll try to follow us in here?"

He hesitated. The last thing he wanted to do was alarm her, but she was sharp enough to see through any false platitudes he could offer. "I'm pretty sure they will. They've gone to a lot of trouble to catch up with you so far." It rankled that neither Cassie or he had a clue why. "Where is Hawk, anyway? What the hell is going on?"

"I wish I knew." Cassie bent suddenly, and then straightened with a long stout stick in her hand. She began walking again, the stick stirring the leaves before her. His stomach clenched as he recognized her intention. She was checking for snakes. Texas had more than a hundred different species, four of them poisonous. And the majority of snakebites happened because people accidentally sat or stepped on the reptiles. He eyed the ground warily. He'd never been overly fond of the creatures.

"He left for North Carolina a couple of weeks ago." Cassie set a good pace as she continued to talk quietly. "He wanted to… He decided to try to find our birth parents."

The news was surprising. Shane had known that

Cassie and her twin were adopted, of course. But though they'd talked often of their adoptive parents, now dead, he'd never heard either of them mention their birth parents.

"What brought on his interest?"

She hesitated, and Shane's instincts sharpened. "Hawk had tried other times to find them, but he always met with a dead end. This time he was determined to follow through until he discovered the truth. And he was able to trace our birth mother. She died when we were infants."

Cassie's stride lengthened. She still didn't know how to feel about the news Hawk had shared with her a few days ago when he'd called. Her adoptive parents had been dead barely three years, her father in a car accident and Mom of a heart attack barely four months later. She and Hawk still grieved. Al and Holly Donovan had never treated them like less than their natural children, and Cassie had rarely spent time wondering where she'd come from.

But discovering the date of their birth mother's death had given the woman substance, made her more real somehow. It had also summoned all sorts of questions for which there were no answers, at least not now. Her brother had shared only a few details, even more reticent on the phone than he was in person, promising to tell her everything once he got home.

"We have another brother. He found out that much. And I look like our mother," she said softly, the words slipping out without planning them. "Hawk found a picture. He's bringing it with him." Just the thought of seeing her real mother's face brought a welter of emotion, none of it easily identifiable. What should she feel for the woman who had given them life, then given them up? Gratitude? Anger? Had she wanted them to have a better life, or had they been a nuisance she couldn't be bothered with?

There was a tug on her coat, and she turned quizzically to meet Shane's gaze. To her shock, he reached out, pushed her hair back, his fingers brushing her jaw with a touch that still sent a quiver of awareness through her. ''Then she must have been exquisite.''

His words surprised her even more than his touch had. But it was his expression that stole her breath. The gleam afforded by his flashlight threw his face into relief. She could see that his features had softened, the way they used to whenever he'd held her. And although she couldn't see his eyes, for just a moment she allowed herself to imagine that a familiar look had stolen into them. The one that said he'd found something infinitely precious, something he wasn't willing to let go.

But he had let go. Shane had given up on her all too easily. In the end he'd walked away without a backwards glance. The stark memory had her eyelids snapping open.

Cassie turned, deliberately stiffening her knees, which seemed to have gone to water. With her fingers tight around the stick, she proceeded to make her way forward again. Because despite the new life they'd created, despite the danger that threatened, nothing between them had changed in the least.

And that was the fact she needed to remember when her heart went all mushy and soft from a single caress. Shane Farhold might be the father of her baby. But that was all he'd ever be to her. All he'd ever let himself be.

"I'm telling you, it'd be better to wait until morning." Jack Nearling stubbed his foot on a rock and muttered a curse. It was stupid to be following this damn broad up the rocky slope after Donovan and the guy. Even dumber to think they could actually make any headway trying to trail them in the forest at night. Did she think he had frigging night vision? The bitch may be some sort of genius, but this plan of hers was plain stupid.

Sheridan whirled on him suddenly, and he couldn't help flinching. He wasn't scared of no broad, but this one... She was more viper than woman. He hadn't mistaken the look in her eye when she'd held the gun on him awhile ago. She was capable of using it. Not only that, but she'd enjoy it. The hair rose on the back of his neck and he took an involuntary step back.

"I'm not willing to wait by idly while they get farther away. We have a flashlight. If you're as good a tracker as you claim to be, that should be enough light to follow them."

He snorted at that, then at her glare turned it into a cough. "Believe me, it's a bit harder than that. And there's no telling how long the batteries will hold out. How are you going to feel about traipsing through the forest at night without a light, huh? Texas has its share of wild animals, not to mention poisonous snakes." He searched her face carefully, but her expression was as flinty as usual.

"We follow them now. I don't want their trail going cold. And I don't mind shooting snakes."

Somehow he didn't think she meant the slithering
kind. There was that look in her eye again, the one
that reminded him of a dog he used to have. Best
damn hunting dog he'd ever owned, until it had gotten a taste for blood. After that it would tear the game
to pieces before Jack could get to it. Sheridan had
that look to her, as if she'd spilled blood before and
would enjoy doing it again.

"Okay, just don't blame me if we're stuck in there
half the night without a light." Silently, they trudged
up to the timberline. It occurred to him that he'd have
Sheridan at his back once they hit the forest, and the
realization didn't sit well. She might pay good, but
he didn't trust her. Not one bit. Once they caught up
with the couple and offed the man, he wouldn't put
it past Sheridan to try to double-cross him.

They'd reached the edge of the forest, and Jack
turned on the flashlight, carefully searching for a clue
to where the two had entered. Maybe it was time for
him to change the game plan. His eye caught a clump
of broken twigs and he went down on one knee to
examine it more closely. Whoever Sheridan was
working for seemed to have plenty of money. Probably wouldn't much care who delivered Donovan to
him, as long as he got the woman. He rose, the idea
filling him with satisfaction. All he had to do was
get Sheridan to tell him who her boss was and where
to find him, and he was in business.

"Did you find something or just decide this was
a good place for a rest?"

His fingers tightened around the flashlight at Sheridan's caustic tone, fantasizing about smashing the
heavy Maglite against her skull. "Something came
this way." He took several more steps, sweeping his

beam around the area. Yeah, he could definitely do this alone. He was the one she was relying on to find the broad and the guy, wasn't he? What the hell good was Sheridan now? Whatever she had in that bag she was guarding so closely, he was sure he could use it on Donovan just as well as she could.

Thinking of the woman they'd come to snatch, his plan began to sound even better. Donovan was a damn fine-looking woman, with that long black hair and green eyes. First time he'd ever seen eyes that color. She was shorter than he usually picked them, not as round, but there had been curves there. Oh, yeah. He felt himself begin to harden at the thought of having that slender, feminine body under his, all that long black hair wrapped around his fists as he pounded into her. He could shoot the man, grab up the broad and have his fill of her before handing her over to Sheridan's boss, collecting the money himself.

He cast a careful eye at Sheridan. First, though, he'd have to get the information he needed from her. It shouldn't be that hard. She wasn't half as smart as she thought she was. And there wasn't a female alive who could outsmart Jack Nearling.

Pressing his palm against his stiff member, he grunted, adjusted himself. Things were going to go his way for once. And when they did, he'd get to screw a hot woman and then make a load of money off of her.

Not a bad reward for a job well done.

Shane shone the light on his watch. He figured they'd been walking about four hours. The vegetation had thinned, at least for the moment, easing their way. They'd taken short breaks for water and to an-swer nature's call, but they hadn't really rested. Each time he'd mentioned it, Cassie had stoutly claimed to be fine and had forged forward again.

Despite her arguments to the contrary, her stride wasn't as effortless as it had been and her shoulders weren't as straight. She was carrying the lightest pack, but he worried that even it would grow heavy as her body grew fatigued. He was just as eager to put as much distance between them and the kidnap-pers as she was, but he wasn't willing to sacrifice her health to do it.

He was just about to propose they stop, as firmly as he needed to, when she halted dead in her tracks, so abruptly that he nearly ran into her. "Good idea," he murmured. "I was just about to suggest..." His voice tapered off as he became aware of the aroma in the air. The distinctive smell of fresh blood.

Looking over her shoulder, he finally saw why she'd stopped. There was a mountain lion not ten feet in front of her, staring directly at them. Tannish brown, it was a full four feet long, with a long, thin tail tipped in black. Beneath it was what looked like the remains of a freshly killed deer. They'd obvi-ously interrupted the cat's feeding, and the animal didn't look particularly friendly.

A warning roar split the air. It didn't sound friendly either.

"Put your hands in the air," Cassie hissed.

"We're surrendering to it?" he asked incredu-lously.

"No, it'll make us look taller. Put them up!"

Shane racked his brain for what he knew about the animals, and came up with nothing. He was a transplant to the area. It wasn't as if they had large wild cats running around the hills of Boston. "So, I take it these guys aren't friendly." He raised his hands slowly, the flashlight and rifle still gripped in them.

"Especially when a kill is interrupted. I'd heard there had been sightings in this area, but no lion population has been documented around here for years."

The lion roared again, giving them a look at a mouthful of very sharp teeth. "I'm willing to document the existence of this one."

"We're going to back up now. Real slow." Shane stepped aside so that Cassie moved even with him, then behind. "C'mon!" she growled, tugging at his pack. In tandem they moved slowly back. The lion didn't appear especially mollified. Its head low, it continued making low, threatening noises and took a few steps forward, snarling.

"If it attacks, fight back. Mountain lions have been driven off by prey that stands and fights."

"Good to know." Shane took another step backward. "Believe me, I have every intention of fighting if it decides to eat us."

"I could shoot it." Cassie's voice sounded steady enough. They continued their odd dance, the two of them moving backward as the cat stalked toward them, its tail twitching. "Hard to miss at this range."

The sound of the shot would immediately pinpoint their location, as well. Both of them knew it. "Let's see if we can avoid that," he murmured. He took his eyes off the lion long enough to search the forest floor for a rock and found one a foot away lodged deeply in the soil. After dislodging it with a few solid kicks, he leaned his rifle against the tree trunk, reached back to shove the flashlight in his pack, then scooped up the rock in both hands.

"I think it's stopping," she whispered. "Maybe it thinks it's scared us off."

"I'm willing to let it go right on thinking that. Grab my rifle and let's head over to the right. We'll give it a real wide berth."

There was a moment when he was convinced she was right. The lion had halted. Shane lowered his hands as they began moving away. Then he stiffened. The cat crouched, snarled again, then sprang.

Shoving himself in front of Cassie, he yelled, "Run." Without looking to see if she'd obeyed, Shane raised his hands again, waited for the animal to get closer, then heaved the rock with all his strength in the mountain lion's direction.

The stone hit the cat squarely on the head, and it screamed hideously. Something sailed by him and caught the animal in the shoulder. A flashlight. Cassie hadn't run, after all. He grabbed his flashlight out of his pack and tossed that, too, catching the lion in the back. It screeched again, before wheeling around and leaping away. Shane took his eyes off it long enough to turn to look at Cassie.

She was just lowering the rifle from her shoulder. "Good aim." Her voice was light, almost disguising the tremble in it. "It'll have a heck of headache tomorrow."

"Have you always been this poor at taking orders?" Relief mingled with irritation in his voice. It didn't escape him that she had a bad habit of staying put when he wanted her far, far away.

"Always." Tentatively, she reached down to retrieve her stick, then picked up the flashlight where it had landed. One was still on, its beam shining into the forest floor. Picking it up, she began to search for the other. "You must have been so dazzled by my charms before that you just overlooked some of my less admirable traits."

Dazzled. Shane considered the word. It was a close enough description for the way he'd felt about her. She'd blurred his guard, confused his senses. There would have been very little that he wouldn't have forgiven her. And yet somehow fate had conspired against him, giving her the one trait he couldn't overlook.

"Here's yours." Her voice interrupted his thoughts. She held up his flashlight, clicked it on for him. Walking over to her, he reached for it, then for his rifle, which she'd set down next to her.

"Chances are it'll be back. It's not going to leave its dinner for long."

"No problem," he said grimly. "I plan for us to be far away from here by the time it does." They veered to the right, keeping well away from the lion's kill.

After a half hour, Shane said, "We can't keep this up all night. Our bodies need to refuel. We're well ahead of them, and they'll have a heck of a time following our trail in the dark, anyway. It won't hurt to take an hour or two to refresh. We'll be able to set a faster pace if we do."

"By 'we' you mean me," she snapped. "I can keep going as long as you can."

Seamlessly, he switched tactics. "Okay, then *I* need to rest." He knew intuitively that he'd get nowhere with her by pointing out that she was barely into her second trimester, a time when most pregnancies had women exhausted by the end of a normal day. This one had been anything but. "I'm jet-lagged and my shoulder is getting stiff."

"Are you in much pain? I threw a first-aid kit in my pack. Does your dressing need to be changed?"

At the concern in her voice Shane shifted uncomfortably, feeling like a fraud for tugging on her guilt strings. It was on the tip of his tongue to tell her the truth, to confess his worry for her, when her words belatedly registered and he stopped in his tracks. "How did you know about my dressing?"

Cassie halted too and gazed at him steadily. For a few moments the rest of the sounds of the forest faded away. "I 'saw' the whole thing, remember? I warned you before you left. You wouldn't believe me then. Maybe you will now."

A bat swooped low, right in front of them. Neither of them noticed. The last thing Shane wanted to discuss with her was the very thing that had driven them apart. He was willing to concede that perhaps manipulation hadn't been her game back then. It was entirely possible that she actually believed in this psychic hocus-pocus she was spouting.

It just wasn't possible that she'd get him to believe it.

"I didn't buy it then, I don't now," he said flatly. Brushing by her, he began to walk rapidly, expecting her to follow.

But the only thing that followed him was her voice, and her words brought him to a halt. "You were traveling at night, driving in a jeep or an open vehicle of some kind. The road you were on was primitive, more of a trail really. The country was rugged, with mountains in the distance. Someone was with you. I don't know who. But a shot rang out, then blood poured from your left shoulder and you fell to the ground.''

The wound she mentioned throbbed at the quiet recital. And a vise in his chest squeezed hard. He swung around to meet her gaze, his mind circling frantically for an explanation. How could she have details of what had occurred halfway around the world? He hadn't given that much information to anyone. Not even Simon. The only one who could have known all that was the woman in the jeep with him, a French nurse named Davida Regald. But as far as he knew, the woman was back in Paris.

"How do you know that?" he whispered hoarsely.

"You tell me, Shane." Her voice was quiet, her gaze intense. "How *could* I know that? I wasn't there. If you say you didn't tell anyone here, then you have to believe what I tried to tell you months ago. I 'saw' it before it ever happened. That's why I didn't want you to go."

Everything inside him rejected her words. His mind grappled for an answer, seized on one gratefully. Davida must have written a report, or told someone back at the base hospital who had sent details to the administration of Greenlaurel Community Hospital, where he worked. If the explanation raised further questions, he was able to quell them for the moment. Someone here had to have gotten those details and passed them on to Cassie.

In the face of his silence, her expression grew stony. "Forget it. It's plain that you'll never admit the existence of something you can't prove scientifically."

"If there's no evidence, it doesn't exist," he said

with more certainty than he was feeling at the moment. Science was soothing with its equations and solutions. Where life had been short on predictability, science had provided security. You couldn't depend on people to be there for you, but gravity remained constant. He might have spent years wondering if his father would ever come home again, but through it all E always equaled mc squared. When his grandmother had turned his young life into a shambles, he'd learned to value the invariable.

He couldn't explain all that to Cassie; he wouldn't have had the words even if he wanted to. But she was already falling in step, with strides as long as if she hadn't been on her feet for nearly twenty-four hours. And he knew she wouldn't have heard him even if he'd been capable of offering an explanation.

After another twenty minutes he pointed his flashlight toward a large boulder. "We can rest there for a while. C'mon." Silently, she followed him. Checking over the area carefully, he finally unrolled one of the blankets and made a mat for them to sit on. Cassie shrugged off her pack, setting it next to the rock. The way she practically collapsed on the blanket told him better than words how exhausted she was.

Now that they'd stopped moving, he was more aware than ever of the noises evident in the darkness. There was still the quiet chirp of insects, despite the fact that it was October. The call of the night hunters echoed in the shadows, eerie reminder of nature's eternal struggle between predator and prey.

Given the events of the last couple hours, he felt a newfound affinity for the latter.

From his pack he took out a thermos and some food. They ate and drank in silence. While he packed things away again, she drew up her knees, rested her forehead against them. But she wouldn't sleep. He knew that, even when he settled next to her, tucking the spare blanket around them both. Her body was too tense, her breathing too shallow. Somewhere in the distance an owl sounded.

"Do you think the world was always round, or not until Galileo convinced everyone it wasn't flat?"

Frowning, he struggled to follow her meaning. "What? It was round, of course."

"And it wasn't so long ago that scientists thought atoms were the smallest form of matter, right?" She raised her head to look at him in the darkness. They'd turned off their flashlights to save the batteries. "But now they know there's something smaller. Quarks, and those lep-thingees."

He smiled in spite of his exhaustion. "Leptons, yes."

"Do you think they'll eventually discover particles even smaller?"

He shrugged, leaned his head against the rock and closed his eyes. "Entirely possible."

"But there's no scientific proof that there's anything smaller. Not yet."

His eyes snapped open again as he started to see where this conversation was going. "There's precedent—"

"Just because something hasn't been scientifically established doesn't mean it's impossible. If man had believed that, the Wright brothers would never have attempted a flying machine. Space would never have been conquered." There was a thread of stubbornness in her voice that almost covered the hurt. "Don't dismiss what can't be proved, Shane. Why can't you accept that maybe, just maybe, there are some phenomena that science can't explain yet?''

His mind rejected her argument even as his heart recognized her plea. Responded to it. He stared into the darkness, thoughts of rest fleeing as memories crowded in. Unwelcome memories, the lot of them. He'd become adept over the years at avoiding thinking about them at all.

Long after Cassie had given up, had put her head down again, he finally spoke, surprising them both. ''When I was nine, my dad took off. Went out for a carton of cigarettes and never came back.'' He smiled without humor. ''Must have been a hell of a smoke. It was tough on my mom. Even working two jobs she never seemed to be able to make ends meet. I can see now that it was desperation that drove her back to find her mother. My grandmother. But it was awhile before I understood why she'd left in the first place.''

Absently, he reached over, rubbed his shoulder, trying to loosen the tightness there. ''Gran is intelligent. Could have been anything, done anything she wanted. But what she enjoys most is running scams.'' Cassie hadn't lifted her head, but he could tell from the stillness of her body that she was listening. ''She's not too particular about which cons she runs, but she leans toward the mystical. The spiritual. The psychic. There doesn't seem to be any lack of people gullible enough to part with a twenty to have their fortune told. Have their aura read. Summon loved ones dead and buried.'' He gave a short laugh. ''God knows she finds them all.''

He'd been excited when she'd asked him to help her, he remembered derisively. The old woman had always known just what buttons to push, and she'd been a master at the controls. He could earn some extra money, help his mom out. It would give him and his grandmother more time to spend together, too. They could make up for all the time she'd missed getting to know her only grandson. He'd fallen for all the excuses. In the end, he'd been as easily duped as the rest of her marks.

"We'd play it different ways. If they came to have their fortune told, I'd go through a purse, lift a wallet. Look for pictures or any other clues about their lifestyle, feed the information to her. I actually enjoyed the spirit-summoning best. I got to run the tapes and a special projector she had. Flashed a damn good impression of a ghost up on the wall. Used to scare even me some of the time."

But he'd known it was wrong, despite his grandmother's assurances that they were making people happy. They were giving them what they wanted. He liked making people happy, didn't he?

"She used you like that?" Cassie's tone was horrified. "Her own grandchild?"

"I don't think she believes to this day that she did anything wrong." He'd failed to find even a hint of a conscience in the woman over the years. "In the end, it caught up with her. When the police came for her, they snatched me up, too." He could still see the small room the detectives had taken him to. Could hear the pointed questions, designed to elicit the most damning information about his grandmother. "They used what they got from me to solidify their case against her. She went away that time, for about a year, more or less. Long enough for my mother to get us far away from her again."

"She… Where is she now?"

"County lockup in Boston." He was tired of the whole story. "Trying to scrape up bail money."

"Being a fake isn't her worst crime, Shane," Cassie whispered. "What she did to you, teaching you not to trust…that was far worse."

He closed his eyes again, suddenly weary. "Go to sleep, Cass." He wished he could follow his own advice, but doubted he would. There were too many specters of the past that refused to be silenced.

Chapter 6

"I can't believe this!"

Hawk Donovan glared out the window of the Raleigh motel as the wind whipped sheets of rain against the glass. Letting the curtain slip out of his fingers, he stalked back to the small table to address the man calmly sipping coffee there. "You're telling me we can't get a charter out of here? The Bureau doesn't even have that much pull?"

"All flights have been grounded because of numerous tornado sightings." FBI agent Liam Brooks sipped, then set the mug back on the table. "Guess the FAA trumps the FBI in cases like this."

They'd been so close. Hawk's fist clenched at his side. If they'd been able to catch that plane Liam had arranged for prior to leaving Wyatt, they'd be in Texas right now. Instead they'd had to hole up in this place to wait out the series of storms plaguing the area, and agonize over what might be happening at the ranch. And the not knowing was driving him crazy.

He shot another look at Brooks. Despite the man's outwardly calm air, he had to be chafing at the wait, as well. The agent was hoping Sheridan would eventually lead him to her boss, Benedict Payne.

Titan.

Just thinking of the man's name was enough to spread a chill through him. And the thought of what Titan would do to Cassie if Sheridan successfully delivered her to him made him break out into an ice-cold sweat.

Sheryl Eldanis picked up Hawk's hand, shoved a mug of coffee in it. "Sit," she said firmly, nudging him toward a chair next to Liam.

Hawk obeyed, but only for a moment. Then he was up pacing again, his coffee forgotten. "We've wasted too much time already. Let's drive. We can take Sheryl's truck, right?"

The petite blonde came up, slipped her arms around him and squeezed. For a moment, worry for his sister gave way to another emotion, instant and compelling. He covered Sheryl's hands with one of his. He hadn't expected to find love when he'd gone looking for his birth parents. She was by far the best discovery he'd made on this journey.

"I know you're half out of your mind with worry," Liam said soberly. "I don't blame you. But we alerted the sheriff's department in Greenlaurel, and we should be hearing from them anytime. In the meantime, waiting isn't something I do well either, but one tornado has already touched down right outside of town. There's supposed to be a string of them hitting all over the state. With the damage they're causing, the roads are likely to be treacherous.''

"Liam said they had an APB out on Sheridan, right?'' Sheryl looked at the agent for confirmation. At his nod, she added, ''She might already have been picked up that way.''

Hawk knew what the two of them were trying to do and he appreciated the attempt. But he was a pragmatic man, one who dealt with reality, no matter how unpleasant it got. With one last absent pat to Sheryl's hand, he broke away to prowl again. "What happens if Cassie gets injected?'' He noted the way Liam's gaze slid away from his, felt his heart sink in response. "The Bureau has its own scientists, right? Couldn't they come up with an antidote?''

"Let's not think of the worst-case scenario." The agent's lack of a straight response was its own answer. "We can't be sure the person Cassie described was even Sheridan. She and her friend could be safe in town right now.''

But Hawk knew better. He didn't have his sister's psychic ability, but the cold lump of foreboding sitting in the pit of his stomach was its own warning. After they'd been cut off, he'd tried several times to call the ranch, and Cassie's cell, to no avail. And if the sheriff had found everyone all right there, they'd have gotten word by now.

"Remember, Cassie isn't alone.''

Sheryl's reminder eased a tiny sliver of Hawk's worry. It was ironic that just a few short weeks ago, Shane Farhold would have been the last man he'd have wanted anywhere near his sister. Hawk had never seen Cassie as desolate as she'd been after the two had broken up. But now the doctor was the only one standing between her and Sheridan. They'd already attributed at least one death to the chemist. Given her relationship with Benedict, there was no telling how many other victims she'd left behind. Given the gravity of the situation, even Farhold's presence was welcome.

He walked to the window again, looked out at the driving rain and tried to send silent strength to his sister.

Hang on, Cassie. I'm coming. Just hang on.

Shane's eyes opened, his body coming instantly alert. Checking his watch, he calculated he'd slept an hour. Maybe less. He'd sat awake long after he'd felt Cassie's body relax next to his. Once her breathing had gone slow and even, he'd given in to the temptation to reach out and position her head against his shoulder. She'd curled up against him so trustingly, so relaxed, that some of the tension inside him had seeped away, a fraction at a time. Finally, he'd slept, too.

She whimpered, moved restlessly. This was what had awakened him, he realized. Dawn hadn't broken yet, but the sky had lightened, heralding its approach. Cassie gave a broken cry, and his gaze went to her. Whatever she was dreaming wasn't pleasant. Small wonder. The past twenty-four hours hadn't exactly been a picnic.

He reached out, meaning to waken her. But before he touched her, her own hands stretched outward, upward. Her whimpering grew louder.

Despite himself, he felt the hair on the back of his nape rise in response. Her arms were raised in a defensive stance, as if to ward off a blow. Her breathing grew more labored, until she was gasping for air. Growing increasingly concerned he reached out and shook her sharply. "Cass, wake up."

But she didn't waken. Whatever nightmare had her in its grip wasn't ready to let go. Not yet. He thought for a moment that she'd stopped breathing. Her arms fell limply to her sides. Moving aside, he lowered her to the ground, checked her airway, found it clear. "Cassie," he said as loudly as he dared. "Wake up." He shook her shoulder, and after a moment her eyelids fluttered open.

A measure of relief filled him. He watched her carefully, observing the huge gulps of air she was taking. Reaching out, he picked up her wrist, felt her pulse galloping. "How do you feel?"

He didn't think he was imagining her disoriented air as she straightened, belatedly pulling her hand away from his. Nor the trembling of her fingers as she pushed them through her hair. "Fine. I'm fine. Just a dream."

She didn't look fine. She looked like a woman trying mightily to pull herself together, to avoid flying into a million tiny pieces. "Some dream."

She lifted a shoulder, the movement jerky. "I've had it since I was a kid." Struggling to her feet, she bent to retrieve the blanket. He stepped aside so she could shake it, then watched as it took her four attempts to roll it up again.

"Do you want to talk about it?"

"What?"

Her flat tone was its own answer. Still he pursued it, unable to help himself. "This nightmare that keeps recurring. It seems to be a doozy. What's it about?"

"Murder."

The stark reply had him freezing. She attached one bedroll to her pack, then went to work on the other blanket. "Whose murder?"

This time she did look at him, and her eyes... Her eyes still held glimpses of horror in their depths. "Mine."

When she would have gone back to tidying their gear, he rose, went to her side and pulled her up to him with a hand to her arm. "Cassie, if you've been troubled by this nightmare for a long time, maybe you need to see someone. Talk to someone to find out what it means."

"I know exactly what it means." Her voice was lifeless. "I've always known." Disengaging herself from his grip, she bent, handed him his pack. Because he couldn't think of what else to do, he took it.

"There are doctors who specialize in sleep disorders," he offered. How often was she bothered by this, he wondered? She'd never mentioned having nightmares before and he'd never witnessed her having one when they'd slept together. But then, they'd rarely spent much time sleeping.

"Ah, science again." Her voice was mocking. "This isn't something science can cure. All the medications in the world, all the shrinks in the country can't prevent the inevitable from occurring."

With her words, comprehension began to creep in, a little at a time. "You can't believe..."

"I've never had a dream that didn't come true." He wondered if she could hear the cold bleakness that crept into her tone. "Not ever. Not when I dreamed about what kind of foal Sultan would throw. Not when I dreamed of Hawk breaking an arm falling out of the hay mow. Not when it's you, shot in a foreign country in the middle of the night. They all happen, Shane, and there's nothing that can change that.''

She turned away, reaching into her pack to withdraw her flashlight. Then with a swift motion, she swung the backpack onto her shoulder.

''For God's sake, Cass.'' He could only imagine the suffering she'd undergone, believing what she did. And a part of him was ashamed. Three months ago he'd accused her of manufacturing that story in an attempt to manipulate him into staying. He'd been down that road before, or one close enough like it. But he could see now that whatever these dreams were, she believed in them implicitly. And he was helpless to soothe the kind of despair they must cause her.

She turned to look at him, her gaze stripping him bare, exposing the twisted welter of emotion he was grappling with. ''Promise me something.''

''What?''

''You said you'd be there for him...for the baby. Do you still mean that?''

''Of course.''

''When...'' She hesitated, but not before he understood what she'd been about to say. ''If something happens to me...you'll raise our baby?''

His chest squeezed tightly. ''Nothing's going to happen to you.''

But her gaze was unswerving. ''Do you promise?''

And because he could tell how important it was to her, he felt himself nod. ''I promise.'' He saw some of the tension stream out of her. Without planning to, he said, ''And, Cass? I don't think it's a him.''

She looked at him, her brow furrowed. "The sono-grams can be tricky, but it sure looks like a baby girl to me."

For some reason she seemed stunned. "A girl?" she whispered.

His heart, his throat, were full. "Yeah. I'm going to put in a request for dark hair and green eyes. I've developed a weakness for the combination."

Tears sounded in her voice. "A baby girl."

He gave a laugh and followed a compulsion. Tugging on her arm, he brought her to him, squeezed her tight. "Don't sound so surprised. I'm told there's about a fifty-fifty chance."

"I know." For one moment she leaned against him, her weight welcome. "There's always a boy in the dream, though. Dark hair. From the connection I feel to him I always assumed…"

"It's just that—a dream. It's not real."

Immediately he knew it was the wrong thing to say. He'd have known it even if her body hadn't gone stiff again, if she hadn't straightened and moved away from him. He felt a flare of anger. He couldn't pretend to believe something that he didn't. Although he could sympathize with whatever was troubling her, he couldn't embrace it. And he knew, as she snapped on her flashlight and started through the forest without another word, that the distance between them hadn't been spanned in the slightest.

If anything, it yawned even greater than before.

They ate again at daybreak, stopping only long enough to relieve themselves before heading out again. Cassie consulted the compass frequently, making calculations in her head. They were still a good

distance south and west of where she thought they'd
find the cabin. But if they continued in this direction
awhile longer, the terrain would get a great deal rockier. They could travel the rocks for a while, in an
effort to throw the kidnappers off their trail.

When she suggested the idea to Shane, he agreed.
Her body was less enthusiastic. Although she would
have denied it if asked, her legs had taken on the
consistency of cooked noodles. She got a heck of a
workout every day training the horses, but hiking always took a whole different set of muscles, and every
one she had right now was protesting. Making their
way across a forest floor that had grown increasingly
dense again was arduous. The bottoms of her jeans
were already torn and frayed from the contact with
the thorns and saw briar that seemed to grow everywhere. Shane didn't look much better.

Shane. She didn't want to think about him, or
about the scene a couple hours earlier. He couldn't
have made it any plainer that he thought she was
crazy. His reaction shouldn't have surprised her.
Wasn't this exactly why she'd never shared her ability with anyone besides Hawk?

But it was one thing to realize how other people
would react to the news. It was another to have that
reaction slapped in her face by the man she'd loved.

It would be easier, far easier, if she could still feel
anger. Resentment. Betrayal. But the emotions were
difficult to summon after what he'd revealed last
night. It was all too easy to understand the confusion
a small boy must have felt to be used the way he
had by his own grandmother. To imagine the guilt
he'd felt at being forced to give evidence against her.
It was difficult to be angry at him when she could

see so clearly now what had shaped his perceptions. The only thing left to feel was disillusionment. There was no common ground for them. She could accept that now, even as a part of her mourned. He could no more deny that which had formed the core of his beliefs than she could turn away from her ability. The only bond left between them was that of their daughter.

Their daughter. A sense of wonder filled her at the thought. Somehow she'd never imagined the baby would be a girl. But perhaps she should have. Cassie suddenly remembered the gypsy from the county fair. The woman had mentioned a daughter, hadn't she? At the time Cassie had focused only on the gypsy's cryptic words of caution aimed at Shane. They had so closely patterned her own fears for him.

"Cassie."

At Shane's quiet voice, she whirled around, certain he was going to warn her of some as yet unseen danger. Instead he jerked his chin skyward. Following the direction of his gesture she looked up, felt her lips curve. There, against the pink grandeur of the spilling dawn, was an eagle, wings fully extended, gliding over the treetops with ease. As they stood watching, it was joined by a second. The duo did several wide slow circles overhead before soaring away as if by silent command.

Every year bald eagles migrated to Texas, although it was still a bit early for the nesting season. Most made their homes around rivers, lakes and reservoirs. And they mated for life. Cassie swallowed, her throat suddenly tight. For an instant she envied the birds their dedication to each other.

Then, without a glance at the man standing silently at her side, she began walking again.

Hours later, Shane stopped her for another short rest. He'd been insisting on more frequent stops today, pressing food and water on her. Cassie ate a little each time, knowing that she had to keep her strength up. But she sipped from the water sparingly. There was no telling how long they'd be in the forest, and even if they found a creek, it wouldn't be safe to drink from it.

She suspected he arranged the stops for her benefit, but didn't comment because she imagined they did him as much good as they did her. After the trauma his body had undergone in Afghanistan, she worried about the stress this adventure was putting on him. Had he fully recovered? It was difficult to tell from looking at him and she knew without asking that she wouldn't get a straight answer.

Cassie sent him a sideways glance. She recalled in vivid detail every fragment of the dream she'd had about him being shot. But nothing in it had indicated how he would have come by the scar zigzagging down his throat.

It was thin, slightly raised, and still pink, partially covered now by day-old whiskers. And imagining how it might have happened had nausea churning in her stomach. She was certain it hadn't been an accident.

Meaning to ask him, finally, about it, she opened her mouth to say, ''How did you—'' His raised hand stopped the sentence before it could be fully completed. Annoyance was her first response, but a moment later she noted his still, listening air, his head cocked to the side. Without thinking, she strained to listen, too, although she couldn't have said to what.

A moment later she heard it, and felt her skin going cold. Voices.

Her heart began to pound. The sound was some distance away. It was impossible to make out words, or even different speakers. She felt panic mix with disbelief. Had the kidnappers caught up with them already? How was that possible?

On the heels of that thought came another that had hope rising and panic receding. "Maybe it's a hunting party," she whispered. "We could get some help, if it is. A bunch of guys with guns definitely would shift the odds in our favor."

"Maybe." The caution in his tone was unmistakable. "But I want to get closer, see what's going on before we call any attention to ourselves. If they're hunters, they've been pretty unsuccessful so far. We haven't heard any shots."

"It could be bow season." She couldn't be sure, because she'd never paid much attention. No one in her family hunted. Hawk, with his special affinity with animals, would rather cut off his arm.

"Why don't you wait behind that oak?" he said. "I'll go on ahead and check things out."

Cassie would have laughed out loud if she could have afforded to make that much noise. "You're not going anywhere without me."

Imperturbably she returned his glare. "If it's someone who can help us, great. If it's not, you can use backup. Either way, we go together."

Evidently recognizing that it was useless to argue with her, he nodded. "Stay in back of me and keep down."

She obeyed without comment. But she did as she was told. Together they moved toward the source of the sound, pausing occasionally to get their bearings, adjust their direction. But slowly, inexorably, they drew closer.

There were several people gathered ahead, Cassie could make out that much. Different voices could be discerned, although the words still were mostly indistinct. She and Shane continued on, each taking care to step lightly.

Finally they came within sight of what looked to be a crude camp. Cassie's heart leaped. The scattered tents meant they were campers or hunters, and either group might be able to help them. There were several picnic coolers, and two men were toiling over cookstoves. Another was fiddling with a small LP gas tank. Mason jars, plastic tubing and what looked like a garden hose lay at his feet.

And all of the men were armed.

No, these weren't typical hunters. Cassie didn't need Shane's frantic gestures to understand that. Rather than rifles or shotguns each of the men carried a handgun of some type. Together she and Shane began to retreat, as quietly as they'd approached. She caught his eye, pointed to the right and he nodded. They began to make their way to the west of the strangers. They didn't speak until they were well away, and then only in low voices.

"Whatever they were up to back there, it wasn't legal." At first Cassie had wondered if the men were poachers, but there had been no hint of any carcasses in the area.

"Drugs would be my guess. Looked like they were manufacturing meth."

As soon as Shane mentioned the idea, Cassie realized he was probably right. She'd heard more than one story of hunters or campers stumbling upon abandoned labs. Some were found in forests, like this one, others in deserted rural buildings, or even in roadside ditches.

"It can be a real hazard for anyone who comes upon the mess they leave behind," Shane said grimly. "The coolers are used as evaporation canisters for the cooking process, which results in extremely toxic phosphorus gas. Some unsuspecting person pulls that lid open and he's surrounded by a cloud of vapor. Anyone in the vicinity can suffer immediate irreversible brain damage. Or worse."

It was another couple hours of hiking before the ground began to get even rougher. She stopped Shane to point out the terrain ahead. "I was thinking we could climb those rocks. It'll be difficult going for a while, but if we could manage it for a mile or so, we should be able to throw off anyone following us."

He stopped to squint in the direction she was pointing. "It'd slow them down anyway," he agreed. Then he swept her with a searching gaze. "But are you up to it?"

"Me?" As if to deny her screaming muscles, Cassie straightened her shoulders. "Stick with me, city boy. I can keep this up for days."

"Let's hope we don't have to." He continued to look at her, clearly unconvinced. "I can't deny that I'm worried about what this is doing to you."

"Physical activity is good during pregnancy." First carefully inspecting the trunk of a nearby tree, she leaned against it.

"There's a difference between going about your regular routine and taking up cross-country hiking," he disputed, concern on his face. "Maybe we should slow our pace. Take more breaks."

"If we break any more often we'll come to a total stop. We have to keep moving." She returned his gaze steadily. "We both know that we have to put as much distance between us and the kidnappers as possible. They'll be making good time today, unless we got incredibly lucky and the lion took care of them for us."

He gave a halfhearted smile. "Something tells me it wasn't in any mood to be doing us favors when we parted."

"All the more reason we keep walking, then."

Clearly torn, he hesitated. But there was no choice, and he must have realized it. Finally, he gave a terse nod. "I'll go first on the rocks and help you climb." When she opened her mouth to protest, he gave her a look to suppress it. "I'm not taking a chance with you or the baby, Cass. You'll let me help, or we'll take an easier way."

She shrugged. "Fine." But there was nothing nonchalant about the ribbon of pleasure that unfurled within her. Whatever the problems between them, she was beginning to believe that his concern about the baby was real, stemming from personal interest rather than a medical one. And that knowledge was more warming than it should have been.

The climb was grueling. Shane knew that he'd never get Cassie to admit it, but his help was not only welcome, but necessary. Although the ground was more sloped than steep, the sheer stamina it took to climb from rock to rock, finding toeholds, took more energy than even he had imagined. They developed a sort of teamwork as they stepped from one rocky ledge to another.

But she never complained, never gave an indication that she was growing fatigued, although he knew she had to be getting exhausted. It was up to him to gauge her flagging energy level, and he was already scanning ahead, looking for a good place for them to break, when he heard a slight sound behind him.

Turning, he held out his hand, intending to pull her up to. his position and then insist on a rest. But once he caught a look of her face, he sprang to her side instead.

She was weaving a little, her eyes wide and unfocused. And when he called her name, twice, she didn't answer. She was mumbling something over and over, and he strained to make it out. ''Snake.''

Sweeping his arm around her waist, Shane guided her to a large flat rock and sat her down on it. Squatting before her, he tilted her chin, peered at her pupils. It was clear she wasn't focused on anything around them.

''C'mon, baby. Snap out of it. Cassie!'' His voice sharpened, but it was still long moments before awareness returned to her eyes, as she turned a puzzled look at him, and then at her position on the ground.

''That's it, we're getting you somewhere you can lie down.'' Resolve stiffened inside him. That was twice now that he'd witnessed her having a spell like that, and it worried him more than he wanted to admit. Although it might well be attributed to the stress she was under, at a time of hormonal upheaval from pregnancy, he'd feel better once he'd had her thoroughly examined by her doctor. Barring that, allowing her body some real rest was going to have to do.

He took off his pack, intending to withdraw the water, when she rose, swayed drunkenly and nearly toppled them both over. "Snake," she said again. Pulling at his arm, she tried to move him. "We have to get out of here."

Glancing around, he couldn't see a reason for her urgency. "Relax. This area is clear." Even he knew enough to realize that snakes liked to sun themselves on the warm rocks, but he'd been watching carefully where he stepped. He hadn't spied one the whole trip.

"We have to leave." When she tried to move him again, he indulged her, intent on finding a place she could lie down. But his foot slipped as he stepped back from her, and he muttered a curse, struggling to regain his balance.

As if in slow motion he saw her reach out a hand. He avoided it, afraid he'd pull her down with him. Instead when the ground gave way beneath his foot, he grabbed for a rock to break his fall, felt the skin scrape away, and a flash of pain in its wake.

Blood made his hand slick and his hold slipped. He took the brunt of the fall with his chest, then his knees, before rolling to a stop several yards away. He could hear Cassie's voice coming to him as if from a distance, the urgency registering, even if her words didn't. He lay there for a moment to get his bearings, taking inventory of a chorus of assorted aches as they made themselves known. It was a moment before he straightened, then gingerly rose. Cassie's voice sounded again, and comprehension dawned at the exact moment he saw what she was screaming about.

There was a snake, coiled and rattling not a foot away from him. And even as he backpedaled wildly, felt himself falling, he saw a blur of motion as it struck.

Chapter 7

There was a blast, a little too close to Shane for him to be entirely comfortable. By the time his vision cleared and his ears stopped ringing, Cassie had dropped her gun and was half-climbing, half-sliding down the slope toward him. Words tumbled from her lips.

"Are you all right? Did it bite you? Where do you hurt? Dammit, Shane, *answer me!*"

"Yeah. I don't know. Everywhere." He answered her questions in order, grimacing as he picked himself up. He halted, his eyes widening when he saw the limp body of the snake, not a foot away from him. A violent shudder worked through him. God, he *really* hated snakes.

It was another moment before he noticed that the reptile was headless. He gave a thready whistle. "Nice shot, Annie Oakley."

"Be careful. Even a severed head can still inflict

venom.'' As she closed the distance between them, he scanned the area suspiciously. Severed snake heads. Just the stuff that nightmares were made of.

''I don't see it.'' And he was looking pretty damn carefully. ''I doubt there's much left of it, from the range you fired.''

She dropped to her knees before him, running her hands up and down his calves. ''Are you sore anywhere? Usually they hit the toe or ankle area, but occasionally they can strike higher. Take off your boots and jeans.''

His brows climbed. ''This is kind of sudden. You used to at least kiss me first.'' There was a chorus of complaints from various parts of his body that had taken the brunt of his slide down the hill, but he didn't think he'd been bitten.

She looked up then, her jaw agape, before her eyes began to spit fire. ''You think this is funny, Farhold? Have you ever treated a rattlesnake-bite victim?''

''I once treated an idiot whose pet python wrapped him in a bear hug. Does that count?''

She muttered something about idiots that had nothing to do with his story and everything to do with him. ''Hang on to my shoulder and lift your foot,'' she ordered, rapidly untying his hiking boot. Because he thought it was safer to do as she said, he obeyed. ''There are no puncture holes in the leather.'' She seemed relieved, talking more to herself than to him. After a couple tugs she had his boot off and his sock stripped away, then examined his foot and ankle carefully. She pushed up his jeans, ran her fingers delicately over his calf. Feeling her touch again, even impersonal as it was, was a jolt to his system. It was all too easy to remember the times they'd explored each other's body languorously, until touch ignited the passion that had always been too ready to combust between them. His body reminded him, uncomfortably, that its reaction to her hadn't changed, despite everything that had passed between them.

"It looks okay." Relief laced her voice as she helped him pull on his sock and roll down his pant leg again. He shoved his foot back into his boot before she tugged off the other one and repeated the process. "You got lucky." Releasing a shuddering sigh, she rose, then balled up her fist and punched him in the stomach.

"Hey!" Fixing her with a reproachful look, he rubbed the area, which stung more than he'd ever admit. "Disappointed that the snake didn't finish me off? Trying to complete the job?"

"You could have died!" He watched, fascinated, as her reaction set in. Her jaw was clenched tightly against the tears he knew she hated to shed. There was a sheen in her eyes, though, that told him how close she was to crying. "I've got an antivenom kit in the first-aid pack, but those things only extract about half the venom. You'd still have needed to go to a hospital. And how would I have gotten help for you, huh?"

"I wasn't bitten and I'm not going to die," he reminded her. "Everything's all right, thanks to your sharpshooting skills."

"What if my aim had been off? Everything happened so fast. I wasn't even sure I'd hit the damn thing. I could have missed completely, or—or shot you, or—"

"But you didn't." Because he didn't know of any other way to calm her, he reached out and hauled her into his arms. Her body was stiff against his at first, so he squeezed tighter. After a moment her arms went around his waist, and she returned his hug fiercely. "It's all right. No harm done."

"What about the sound of the shot?" Her voice was muffled against his coat. "Do you think those drug guys or the kidnappers—"

"We're over two hours away from the druggies." He rubbed his face against her hair. "And farther than that from the kidnappers." He spoke with more certainty than he felt. "Even if they could pinpoint our location, by the time either could get here, we'll be long gone."

"I guess." She took a long, shuddering breath and released it.

"If you're looking for something to bandage, though, you can start with my palms."

She jerked away from him, her expression filled with such sudden concern that he would have given anything to have phrased the words differently. "I'm okay. They're just scraped. I need to get them cleaned up."

Immediately she had both his hands in hers, sympathy in her eyes replacing the tears that had threatened earlier. "Well, it doesn't look like something that will keep you out of surgery long term, but they have to sting."

"A little, yeah."

Cassie shrugged out of her backpack and squatted before it, digging inside for the first-aid kit. With a triumphant flourish she pulled it out, and then came back to him. "Hold them out, palms up," she ordered.

Shane thought he could have probably tended his

hands himself, more quickly and efficiently, but having a beautiful woman fuss over him wasn't exactly a hardship. So he remained still for her ministrations, refraining from offering a critique on her nursing skills. What she lacked in technique was more than made up for in attractiveness, at any rate.

He studied her while she had her head bowed over his hands, her lip caught firmly in her teeth as she concentrated on her work. He was male enough to notice a pretty face, but had never fallen for one before. But Cassie was different, had been from the first. Beauty bored quickly if it wasn't backed up with something more intelligent, more alive. Although it might have been her looks that had captured his attention, it had been her incredible energy that had held it. The combination of capable horsewoman and femininity had intrigued him. And he'd been fascinated by the haunting sadness that he'd caught glimpses of.

There had been a time when he attributed that sadness to the deaths of her parents. But in light of what she'd revealed to him earlier that day, the cause went much deeper. How did he console someone convinced that her own murder was imminent? Just the thought sent his senses scrambling. Logic had failed miserably. This wasn't something he could cure with medicine or skill. He was helpless in the face of her burden, and helplessness had always infuriated him.

He could smell her shampoo as her head remained bent before him, something familiar, fresh and lemony. Shane knew how silky it would feel, draped over his chest, caught in his hands. He remembered…too much. The baby-soft skin that covered the inside of her wrists, the pulse below her ear. The way her breath would hitch when he'd catch her nipple between his teeth; the way her fingers would tighten in his hair, pressing his mouth closer.

"I'm happy to report the patient is going to live." Cassie snipped off the tail of the gauze she'd wound generously around his second hand, and tied it neatly. Looking up at him, she continued, "I always wanted to be able to say..." Her voice tapered off, her eyes widening, and he knew that everything he remembered was showing on his face. And he knew she remembered, too.

Without conscious thought he reached for her, and she swayed into his embrace. It was instantly different from the one a few minutes earlier. That had been to soothe and comfort, a celebration of the narrow escape from danger. But this... This was a danger from an entirely different source, one that beckoned seductively. And even knowing just how badly he could get burned, he was helpless to turn away from its allure.

He slanted his mouth over hers, sank into the kiss. It was like coming home. Shane pressed her mouth open, her familiar flavor its own enticement. A rollicking band of pleasure beamed through him, starting a fever in his blood that heated his entire body. It had been like this every time. An instantaneous hunger for more. A craving in the system that was every bit as addictive as any drug.

She twined her arms around his neck, her fingers sliding into his hair. Her tongue met his, a languid velvet slide that teased and tempted. Her taste seared through him, sizzling nerve endings and hazing the senses. This had always been the one time he couldn't summon reason. When control, so well crafted, became a battle he was never interested in winning.

Because of their bulky coats, it was difficult to get close enough. He wedged one leg between hers, let go of her only long enough to slide his arms inside her coat and around her narrow waist and lifted her to him. As quickly as his need had deepened, she'd matched him every step of the way. She'd always done that, he remembered. Met him squarely, kiss for kiss, rising passion for rising passion. She'd fed his hunger, deliberately stoked it and reveled in their blazing desire.

He nipped her bottom lip, just one quick brush of teeth before his tongue swept in to soothe and excite. Tongue and teeth clashed as the angle of the kiss changed, both of them losing their grip on the slippery slope into need.

Her hands were in his coat, her fingers raking his back. The evidence of her hunger fed his own. His mouth moved to her jaw, dropping a string of kisses there. Her throat arched, and he cupped the back of her head with one hand, pressed it to his shoulder to give him better access.

And then he winced, swore, as needles of pain stabbed through him.

Instantly, Cassie raised her head, blinking to regain her focus. "What? What's wrong?"

There was a drugged, dazed look in her eyes that had him reaching for her again. He wasn't ready to relinquish this intoxication. But she leaned back in his arms, searching his face carefully. "Shane? You're in pain, I know it. What's wrong?"

With a great deal of reluctance, he let her go. He could have told her that the pain that came from releasing her was ten times that which his shoulder was giving him. He didn't think it was a subject she'd appreciate.

"I must have opened the wound during my graceful descent down the hill."

She pushed his coat aside, and her face blanched. Looking down, he noted his blood-dampened shirt and mentally cursed. Then Cassie was yanking the shirt from his waistband, fingers flying as she undid the buttons until she'd bared his skin to the fall air.

Blood was oozing sullenly through the gauze dressing, he noted, but it didn't appear too bad. He must not have reopened it completely, just abraded it by his fall.

"Oh, my gosh." Already Cassie had bent to the kit at her feet, rising again with a small pair of scissors in her hand. Quickly, she snipped at the edges of the tape that held the pad in place. But he knew there was only one way to remove it.

Her gaze caught his. "This is going to hurt."

"Then maybe you'd like to do it slower, make it last." He barely managed to stifle a yelp when she yanked the tape free.

"I'm sorry, I'm sorry, I'm sorry."

His heart softened when he heard the concern in her voice. She could never stand to see another person, or even an animal, in pain. "It's okay, Cass. Just open another pad, would you?" Any pain in his shoulder paled in comparison to that emanating from a lower part of his body. He drew a deep breath, silently ordering his disappointed hormones to quiet.

He wiped away the worst of the blood with the edges of the soiled pad, took the supplies from her and smeared first-aid ointment all over the fresh pad.

He hadn't brought his medications with him on the trip to the ranch. The pain pills he could do without. He'd only had that prescription filled in case the constant throbbing kept him awake. But the threat of infection was always real. He made sure only the sterile bandage touched the area around the injury, holding it in place while Cassie secured it with tape. Then he rebuttoned his shirt while she replaced items in the first-aid kit and shut it.

"Whatever happened to my gun?" He just now remembered it. Looking around, he didn't see it anywhere. Some outdoorsman he'd make.

"You dropped it when you fell. Mine's up there, too, along with my stick."

Together, they climbed with new caution back to the area where they'd started. Once they'd retrieved their things, both of them stood there for a moment. Cassie didn't appear eager to meet his gaze.

"We should get going." It wasn't her words, but the finality in them that told Shane she'd just as soon forget what had passed between them minutes ago. He was tempted to push it, but goading her into admitting that she'd felt as much as he had wasn't going to accomplish anything.

"Before I decided to take up cliff-diving, I'd meant to find a place for us to rest."

She turned, began stepping over rocks. "We stopped long enough. After making as much noise as we did, I'll feel better if we head out, get some distance from this place."

Shane had the feeling she was talking as much about their kiss as she was their location, but he couldn't fault her logic. He caught up to her and took the lead so he could help her up the rocks. The fact that she tolerated his action without balking told him clearly how distracted she was.

They walked in silence for a while, Shane, with a newfound wariness, kept an eye out for snakes. He wasn't overly anxious to broaden his experience with them. That thought beckoned another. He looked at her. "Did you see that snake before I did?"

Her face went instantly wary. "What do you mean?"

He frowned, trying to sort out the series of events as they'd happened. "I thought you were going to faint for a moment, before I went down. You were really out of it. The only thing you said was 'Snake.' Did you see it? Hear it?"

Cassie shook her head, keeping her eyes cast down, pretending interest in where she was placing her feet. She'd "seen" the snake, all right, in another of those eerily accurate flashes into the immediate future. But she was loathe to share that particular explanation with Shane.

After their last conversation about her ability, how could she ever expect him to believe this? She was still having difficulty with it herself.

With a creeping sense of trepidation, she wondered how often she could expect the precognitive episodes. She hadn't finished her tea last night, and it would have been useless to pack the ingredients before they'd left, even if she remembered it. She could hardly ask Shane to stop and light a fire so she could boil water with which to mix the ingredients.

But she'd already noticed yesterday that the scenes were clearer, stronger and more frequent when she missed taking the recipe. What she hadn't realized until now was that every one of them had been a forewarning of danger of some kind.

She tried to recall each of the times she'd suffered from one of the spells. When they'd first started, things had been more hazy. She'd blamed it on dizziness from too much sun or getting to her feet too fast. But as the weeks had progressed, Hawk had gotten concerned. He'd told her that she "just went blank" when one occurred. She'd have to take his word for it. She'd never been able to remember the moments leading up to, nor directly following, each incident.

She frowned, gripping Shane's hand strongly as he pulled her up beside him. Recently there had been the snake. The bullet through the living room window. The strange premonition about the couple on her porch. She shuddered. At the time it had been hard to imagine why the man and woman should have made her so uneasy, but it wasn't difficult to understand it now. Not with the deadly intent that Hawk had ascribed to them.

The memories rushed in, one on the heels of another. She could recall the time she'd clearly seen Baby, Hawk's dog, wounded by a bullet meant for him. He'd yet to explain how a hunt for their birth parents had put him in such danger. Before that there had been instances less threatening. Like knowing the new half-wild stallion was going to attack their prize stud when one passed before the other; "seeing" the tire blow out on the truck Jim was driving to town; knowing the barbed wire was going to snap where it was stretched too tight, gashing one of their hired men before he could jump out of the way.

Though it had been weeks since she'd figured out

what was happening, she still didn't know why. Still couldn't understand how her precognition would change how it manifested itself and find a new way to portend threats.

All Cassie knew for sure at this point was that the man next to her wouldn't accept it. Her skin heated as she thought of the kiss they'd shared, half-dismayed to realize just how little had changed between them. But if the passion remained unaltered, so did other things, as well.

Shane Farhold was no closer than before to accepting the ability she'd lived with all her life. And she wasn't about to give him another chance to reject her for it.

Dusk was seeping into the sky, and the sun was casting long shadows as it faded into the treetops in a glowing ball of fire. The sight was lost on Janet Sheridan, however. She'd never been one to enjoy communing with nature. Nor, she thought viciously with a sidelong glance at the man beside her, did she enjoy wasting precious time with idiots.

"You've lost them. Why don't you just admit it?" The cold stale coffee from the truck had long since been drunk. She was hungry and thirsty, and every muscle she had was screaming. As far as she could tell, they were no closer than before to finding Donovan. She had only the word of the cretin at her side that they were even on the right trail.

"We haven't lost them. I found that particle from their blanket, didn't I? I'm telling you, we're right on their path. After hearing that shot earlier, I'm even more sure we're headed in the right direction."

"You don't have the slightest idea whether that

shot came from them,'' she snapped. The man didn't
know how lucky he was that she needed him right
now. The knowledge burned, but without him, she
would have no idea how to get out of this damned
forest. Grimacing, she looked at the lengthening
shadows. It'd be night soon. She hadn't enjoyed
tramping through the wilderness in the dark last
night. She wasn't thrilled with the idea of doing so
again.

She considered her options and realized they were
limited. They might starve in this damn place, or be
torn apart by a herd of those wild pigs they'd run
across, but going back to Benedict empty-handed
would mean certain death. One far more hideous than
anything the wilderness could hold.

She swallowed, the dryness in her throat not totally caused by thirst. ''You'd better be right.'' Because it pleased her, she indulged in another brief
fantasy of just how she was going to get rid of this
oaf when the time came. The methods changed each
time she thought of it, but the result remained the
same.

''Shh.'' His whisper interrupted her plans for his
demise. ''Do you hear something?''

Janet listened and was about to berate him for
alarming her for no reason when she heard what he
had noticed. Voices.

A vicious sense of satisfaction curled through her.
Was it possible that they were about to discover their
quarry? Could they be that fortunate? ''Is it Donovan?''

''Can't tell from here.'' But the possibility gave
Jack a renewed sense of purpose. ''We need to get
closer. I'll go up ahead and make sure, and you wait

here.'' The way the woman had of crashing through the area would alert anyone within ten miles of their presence. And he wasn't about to get this close to the prize and have her screw it up.

"We go together."

He grunted. "Then you're going to have to step quietly. Watch where you plant your feet, for God's sake. We know they're armed and I don't especially look forward to having my damn head blown off because you gave us away." Without another word, he began creeping forward, staying low.

Excitement began to course through his veins. He just might be spending this night a lot more pleasurably than the last. He fantasized for a minute about bedding down with Donovan, once he'd offed her buddy and the bitch behind him. Whiling away the nighttime hours sticking it to her would go a long way toward making up for the past few days hitched up with that pit viper, Sheridan.

He dodged for cover behind a nearby tree and stopped to listen. The voices—and there were at least two of them—were getting closer. His palms went damp thinking of how close he was to getting everything he had coming to him.

Of course, he hadn't managed to get her boss's name from Sheridan yet. She evaded the answer, no matter how sneakily he approached the subject. Maybe it was time to get serious. She'd give it up easily enough when he had his gun pressed against her forehead. And if she didn't, there was bound to be some clue in her pockets, that damnable bag she carried or back in the truck.

Yeah, Jack told himself as he moved stealthily forward, he'd find Sheridan's boss one way or another.

And he doubted it would matter to the man that the merchandise Jack brought him was slightly used.

He squinted, trying to make out the scene up ahead. There were a couple tents, people moving around. His fantasies abruptly vanished.

"What is it? Is it them? Do you see Donovan?"

He moved aside to let Sheridan see for herself. "It's just a group of damn campers." She swore viciously.

"Maybe they saw Donovan, though," Jack said. "They might be able to tell us something." Upon closer look, however, he wasn't certain it was worth the risk to ask the men. These weren't ordinary campers, and if he didn't miss his guess, every single one of them was armed.

He said as much, and Sheridan watched the scene before them, a look on her face that he didn't like. "If there's a chance they saw Donovan, we have to talk to them."

Jack was about to refuse. He hadn't signed on to this gig with the intention of having his dead, bloated body found in the woods. He was about to say as much when the woman beside him said, "I think it's best if I go in there."

Relief hit him in a wave. "You?"

"You'd just screw it up," she said. "And chances are, this group is up to no good. They'll be paranoid, and won't believe a woman poses as much of a threat." She took out her gun, exchanged the clip for a full one. The silencer both of them had on their weapons would ensure whatever transpired, would happen quietly.

"Your only job is to cover me," she said. "Think you can manage that much? Follow my lead. And believe me, if you mess this up, there won't be anything left of your body for the wild animals to feed on.''

Without another word she rose, plunged toward the men, stumbling in her haste to reach them. Jack ducked low and waited.

''Oh, thank God,'' he could hear Janet gush as she stumbled toward the surprised men. Jack could see a couple of them reach inside their coats, ready to pull their weapons. ''I've gotten separated from my party and night is almost coming, and I'm so afraid I won't be able to find them in the dark....''

She was good, Jack admitted to himself grudgingly, his automatic ready. He could have told the men that there wasn't a helpless bone in that broad's body, but they seemed to be buying the yarn she was spinning. He could read the body language of the guys, see their shoulders relaxing. They didn't think Sheridan was dangerous. He nearly snorted. If they only knew.

He listened intently, but each man denied having seen anyone else for the past couple days. One of them pointed to the west in response to Sheridan's question about the shot that had sounded earlier that afternoon. A furious sort of disappointment filled him. They didn't know anything! Damn them!

Apparently she had reached the same conclusion. She was backing away, gesturing, telling the men she'd use the remaining daylight to try to find her friends. From the glances exchanged between them, it was obvious to Jack that they might have other ideas for her. He could have wished them luck. Bedding down with Sheridan would be like screwing a piranha.

His eyes widened then, and he fumbled with his gun, sighting it quickly. When one of the men pulled her, Sheridan had pretended to stumble, grabbed her gun from her coat and put a bullet right between his eyes. With the silencer attachment, he didn't even hear the sound of the shot.

He squeezed the trigger, took down another guy reaching for his gun while Sheridan calmly wheeled around and shot a third, who'd already been in the process of raising his arms high in the air. That left the last man, backing away fast with his hands up. Since Sheridan had him covered, Jack rose and made his way swiftly to the campsite.

"Where's your food?" he heard Sheridan demand. The question sparked Jack's interest. It had been far too long since they'd finished the chips and granola bars they'd brought from the truck.

The stranger flipped the cooler lid open and Jack joined him, dropping to his knees in front of it, taking inventory. There were sandwiches, milk jugs of water and what looked like a sack of cold chicken.

"You saw what happened to your buddies," Sheridan said as Jack tore into the bag of chicken. "You sure you didn't see my friends?"

"For God's sake, lady, I didn't see nothing, I swear." The man was on his knees now, his arms raised high, blubbering. Jack bit into a chicken leg, devouring it with a few quick bites. She took a step closer to the man, drilled him between the eyes, then stepped back as the body slumped forward.

"What'd you find?" she called to Jack. Still chewing, he held out the bag of chicken, his eyes glued to the man she'd just killed.

"Load up some bags with food and water. Take a couple of the guns, too, and let's head out."

For a moment, his appetite had vanished. He dropped the half-eaten piece of chicken to the ground. She was searching the tents, no doubt looking for anything they could take with them. Jack moved fast, finding an empty pack in one of the other tents and shoving in some food and water. For some reason, he couldn't prevent his gaze from stealing back to that last body. She hadn't blinked once, not as the man cried and pled for mercy. She'd just shot him, sidestepping around his slumping body.

A chill worked through Jack's body, and it wasn't from the rapidly approaching night air. There was something unnatural about that Sheridan woman. And this should prove as a reminder to him to step warily. It wouldn't pay to underestimate her.

Chapter 8

"We can't afford to spend the night here," Cassie argued. "We'll rest awhile, but we have to start moving again after a couple hours."

"We're staying longer than that," Shane disputed. He'd picked the place very carefully. The oak to their right, with its massive trunk, gave them good cover from one direction. A collection of boulders sheltered them on two other sides. The ground was relatively free of brambles. The area provided a cozy little three-sided shelter of sorts, and was as good a place to stop as he'd seen. As a bonus, the only animals he'd noted in the vicinity were the squirrels running along the branches of the tree overhead.

Seeing the stubborn look on Cassie's face, he said, "We're both dead on our feet. We'll make better time tomorrow if we're fresh. And I'm not trying to put down your navigational skills, but you have to admit that it'll be easier to find our way in the daylight.''

She sat cross-legged on the blanket he'd spread out, letting the pack slip from her arms. She couldn't hide her exhaustion, he observed with concern. Despite the frequent breaks they'd taken, she was weaker than she'd been the night before. He thought if he could get her to agree to sleep, she'd be out in a matter of minutes. He doubted she'd waken before first light.

"Hopefully, those hours we spent trekking over the rocky area will slow them down."

"Absolutely." He set his pack by hers, then lay his rifle down near the blanket. "Remember, the going is as difficult for them as it is for us. Tracking over rocks is bound to be more difficult."

"That was the idea." It was difficult to tell in the near darkness, but he thought her face had brightened. "They won't be able to pick up our trail over the rocks at night. Maybe not at all." She reached into his pack and took out their dwindling supply of food. The deer sticks were gone, as was most of the fruit. There was just the long summer sausage and a few apples left, and they made a pretty pitiful display on the blanket in front of her.

"Maybe we should have saved the rest of that snake," he joked. "I hear rattlesnake is edible."

"Considered a delicacy in some parts around here. And I already thought of that." She reached into her pack to get something that she threw toward his feet. "I cut off the rattle for you to keep as a souvenir."

The thing landed at his feet, or would have, if they weren't a full twelve inches in the air. Comprehension registered before he hit the ground again. "I never realized you were so sadistic,'' he said, picking up the ball of socks she'd tossed at him.

Cassie was doubled over with laughter. "And I never realized you had such an impressive vertical leap. The Dallas Mavericks could use you."

He threw the socks back at her. "How quickly they forget. I'm almost sorry I saved you from that snake. It had its eye on you, you know. I threw myself in harm's way to deflect its attention."

She hooted at that, which he ignored, getting warmed up to the story. "Without my heroics, it would have soared through the air, up that slope, perhaps biting you on your very delectable backside. Being taken with that part of your anatomy myself, I sacrificed my own body, at great personal cost, no less, and this... This is the thanks I get."

She was lying on the blanket, convulsed with laughter. "You missed your calling." She managed the words between fits of hilarity. "You should have been a political speech writer."

It was, he thought, good to see her smiling again, even if it was at his expense. Grinning, he dropped on the blanket beside her. "Speech writer?" He grabbed the hunk of meat, tapped her on the head with it. "How do you figure?"

She wiped her eyes. "Your gift for revisionist history, of course."

"Such wit," he marveled, giving her shoulder a friendly shove. "I should count myself lucky to be stuck in the wilderness with a comedienne."

"Well, if it makes you feel any better, I couldn't eat rattlesnake even if we could cook it. Although I'm told it tastes like chicken."

"I've heard." And he was quite certain he'd have

to be far hungrier than he was right now to discover that firsthand.

Cassie rummaged through her bag and took out a pocket knife. Flipping out a blade, she cut through the plastic protecting the meat, and then began to peel away the paper coating. With swift, efficient motions she sliced several pieces, then turned her attention to one of the apples. Soon she had a small feast arrayed on the blanket between them. It turned out to be the most relaxing meal they'd had since leaving the ranch.

Afterwards she carefully rewrapped the remains and tucked them back in a bag. Even the apple core could entice animals, or worse, leave an unmistakable clue that they'd been there. He passed her the thermos and she drank sparingly, neither of them commenting on the dwindling supply. After he put that away, too, he noted her drooping eyelids and pulled her pack over for her to use as a pillow. "Why don't you get some sleep." Grabbing the blanket from where it was rolled neatly below his bag, he sat down next to her, spreading the blanket over both of them. "That clump of bushes over there looked like wild raspberries. Maybe we'll get lucky and find breakfast there in the morning."

She yawned and snuggled deeper into the bag. "Better than a 7-Eleven. But we aren't still going to be here by morning."

"Okay, then. We'll leave whenever you want." It wasn't a difficult promise to make. He doubted she'd open her eyes again until dawn, anyway. He listened for her breathing to go slow and even. He would have sworn she was sleeping when her voice sounded in the darkness.

"The kidnappers might not even be on our trail, you know. We had a chance to prepare for this journey, they didn't. They may not even have entered the forest after us."

He was unwilling to extinguish that hopeful note in her words. "That's possible."

Silence reigned between them again for a time, before she gave a little sigh. "But Hawk sounded so urgent on the phone. I've never heard him like that before. It had to have been a serious threat or he wouldn't have been so worked up."

Shane remembered too well the real fear in the man's voice. Whoever the people were who'd come for Cassie, he had no doubt about the danger they posed. Although he had no better idea than she did about what was going on, he was certain it was deadly. And he knew they couldn't count on the risk being over. Not by a long shot.

"We'll just keep on being careful, how's that?" He'd made a vow to her brother, he recalled grimly. But it was more than a promise that would keep him committed to her safety. His feelings for her were still a tangle, but he could admit, at least, that they were there, stronger than ever. Their breakup hadn't altered that. Neither had their time apart. He just didn't have a clue what to do about them.

And now there was the baby to consider. His hands went to his shirt pocket, where he'd placed the sonogram picture. Complications abounded between them, and danger surrounded them. When he'd pictured fatherhood, in a nebulous, distant way, he never would have dreamed it would arrive like this. With a woman he didn't understand, claiming abilities he couldn't accept. And no matter how feverishly his mind circled their problems, he was no closer to finding a solution.

Although the daytime temperature had been pleasant, in the sixties, it had dropped steadily as night approached. He felt Cassie shiver beside him and rolled to his side, fitting her against him. Sharing their body heat was the smartest way to battle the brisk air. But spooning was also a great deal more intimate than lying side by side, making it difficult to avoid thinking of their kiss earlier that day.

It was a little disconcerting to discover just how easily the passion between them could be rekindled. A little alarming to find just how hard it had been for him to release her. His memory obligingly supplied him with only too many details of what it had been like to make love with her. The sleek softness of her skin, the long sweep of silky thigh with the taut muscle beneath, the smooth column of her throat, the firm breasts, the tight bottom. He moved uncomfortably. Everything that mattered hadn't been altered in the least. Not the desire between them. Not the reasons they'd parted.

He realized with a flash that walking away from her, as gut wrenching as it had seemed at the time, had been relatively easy. He'd plunged directly into the Doctors Without Borders assignment. Two thousand miles away, he couldn't have sought her out even if he'd weakened. And there had definitely been times that he'd weakened. Times that he'd spent lying on his cot staring at the ceiling of his tent, seeing her face. Imagining talking to her. Touching her.

But even those thoughts had been swept away by the events that had embroiled him there. The brushes with death that had, miraculously, left him alive. The choices he'd made that had left another dead.

It had been difficult to feel much of anything after that.

That kind of emotional numbness had been its own blessing. Now that the feelings had come swarming back, all the anguish, all the guilt, all the remorse had returned tenfold. And it was regret, he'd found, that could haunt a man, robbing him of sleep and depriving him of appetite.

But it was doubt that would eat him alive.

He'd spent an undetermined amount of time staring into the darkness, every once in a while catching sight of a pair of glowing eyes that stared back at him from the interior of the forest. He would have sworn that Cassie was asleep. But her voice came in the darkness, startling him.

"Do you think…" The hesitation in her voice brought his senses alert. "Could… Would any of this we've gone through hurt the baby? The stress, I mean, or missing regular meals, or…any of it?"

"This is all going to be short-term," he assured her, his mouth close to her ear. "None of this would be something your obstetrician would have recommended, but you're going to be fine. The baby is going to be fine. You said you've been having good reports at your checkups."

She nodded, her hair brushing his cheek.

"That's good, then. We'll have you seen again when we get back to Greenlaurel." That time couldn't come soon enough. "I want to get Dr. Godden's opinion on those dizzy spells you've been having." He wouldn't be satisfied until they'd gotten to the bottom of their source. Pregnant women could be more prone to dizziness, even fainting, from any of several causes. But there was even more to Cassie's episodes that worried him.

He could feel the tension creeping back into her body. The way he was curved around her backside, her reaction would have been difficult to miss. "They aren't dizzy spells, exactly. And I have had them checked out. Thoroughly."

"What'd Dr. Godden say about them?"

Cassie's hesitation was its own tip-off. Shane's instincts sharpened. "I had the tests run a couple months ago. Actually, that's when I discovered I was pregnant."

When she said nothing else, he prodded, "And?"

"And nothing." Her voice was flat.

"The tests were inconclusive."

And she was obviously intent on making him pry every detail from her. "So are you going to give me the details, or am I going to have to wait until I get back to the hospital and find out on my own?"

There was an audible sniff. "So much for the patient's privacy act." Silence stretched, filled with tension. Then finally, she said, "Hawk was concerned. These…spells have happened at some inopportune times, and he thought things could get dangerous for me. But I've been assured they have nothing to do with the baby's health. Everything is fine."

"Did they do a CT? An EEG? MRI?" He would have recommended them. That blank staring she did, her unawareness of what was going on around her, the disorientation when she came to again—all were symptoms of petit mal seizures. But their onset was puzzling. There had been no indication of them at all before he'd left.

"All of them. They ran me through every machine they have at that hospital and found nothing."

Somehow he didn't find the news particularly reassuring. He'd be more comfortable with a reason for the episodes, so as to better devise a plan of action. But medicine wasn't always an exact science. "So the test results were normal? That doesn't mean anything, of course, except that they didn't find a cause for any seizure activity."

"I don't believe they're seizures." Her voice was tight. "I tried several different medications and none of them changed anything. They actually increased in frequency. That's finally what caused Hawk to go looking for our birth parents. When the doctors were stumped, and the medications didn't work, he thought if he could find something out about our family history, he might pick up a clue that would help me."

"And did he?"

"He discovered that my birth mother suffered from the same thing when she was pregnant with us. He called me with the ingredients for an herbal tea that was able to control the episodes."

Doubt filled him. "Herbal tea? Cass, these holistic remedies are well and good, but they can't take the place of medication. For one thing, they haven't been tested or approved. Sometimes they're harmless, but other times certain ingredients can interact with other drugs you're on, or cause side effects you hadn't counted on."

"I'm not on any other medication. Nothing worked, remember? And the tea helped immediately. I…" There was that pause again, before she admitted, "I missed a dose yesterday, though. And it wasn't exactly the first thing I thought of when I was packing to leave the ranch.''

"How often do you take it?" He was thinking as a doctor now, striving for objectivity.

"Twice a day. But I wasn't able to finish it last night before you came. There was a bit going on.'' Her voice was dry.

"So you've missed three doses." And so far he'd witnessed her having two episodes.

"And the spells—for want of a better word—have been getting more frequent,'' she admitted lowly. "One happened just before that couple came up to my door. And then there was another before the shot was fired through the window. Again before we saw the snake.''

Snake. He recalled the single word she'd spoken while he'd been trying to rouse her. Odd, because he would have bet she wasn't focusing on anything around her during those moments.

"Are you seeing a pattern here? Anything at all?''

He frowned, puzzling over it. "Do they always happen prior to some sort of danger? Maybe stress triggers them.'' It was possible, perhaps, that her subconscious could be aware of threats before she'd fully comprehended them. He was far from his medical comfort zone on this one, though.

"Except that the danger is rarely to me.'' Wiggling in his arms, Cassie rolled to her other side, her body pressing even more closely to his. She didn't seem to notice. He did. Too much.

"It happened once when Hawk was in North Carolina. I tried to call his cell, to warn him that his dog, Baby, was going to get shot.''

A sudden block of foreboding settled in Shane's stomach. "How would you know that?"

"That's just it. I 'saw' it. I had one of these same spells, and I saw Baby lying there, blood pouring from his flank. Just like I saw the couple showing up on my doorstep, the bullet through the window, and the snake. At first when these things started, it was just the dizziness. I'd see lights and colors, and feel like I was in a wind tunnel or something. But for the past few weeks they've been getting stronger."

"And you've been 'seeing things.'" Shane's voice was blank. Always, always it seemed to come back to this with Cassie. "I thought you only saw the future in your dreams. Now you're seeing it when you're awake, too?"

A certain guardedness colored her tone. And something that sounded suspiciously like hurt. "About five minutes into the future. I don't know why my precognition would be taking on a different form now. All I know is that it has, and that these episodes haven't taken the place of my dreams. They're in addition to them."

Desolation hollowed out his chest. His memory conjured up words from the past that were eerily similar. *I have a gift, Shane. I can see the past and the future. Isn't that fun? What kind of person would I be if I didn't use my abilities to help everyone I can?*

The only one Genevieve had helped, of course, was herself. She'd fleeced enough of the unwary to always have a tidy little nest egg put away, enough to help her disappear when the police took too much of an interest in just what sort of services she was offering. As an adult he would have been tempted to say that anyone who went to a charlatan like his grandmother was getting exactly what they deserved.

Except that he'd seen, often enough in his time with her, that not everyone who came through her door was a tourist looking for a new experience to talk about back home. He'd been able to observe more than once the fervid hope in their eyes, the suffering in their expression. And he'd known, even then, that her claims weren't harmless.

"I'm guessing you haven't shared any of this with the medical staff at Greenlaurel Community Hospital." His voice, when it came, sounded rusty to his own ears.

"Wise choice, wouldn't you agree?" Her face was tilted up toward his, her words mocking. "Hawk always warned me to not mention my ability to others. He said it made me different, in a way that no one else would understand. He was right. You're the only person I ever told, and it didn't take you long to walk away from me, did it?"

Guilt rose, fanged and punishing. "I don't know what to say to you." And he wished he could at least give her words. "But know when I left, I wasn't rejecting you. I just couldn't handle this…ability you keep talking about."

She stared at him for a long time, and he wanted, more than was comfortable, to reach, cup her jaw, offer *something* to make up for that which he couldn't give her.

But then she rolled away, presenting her back to him in a way that told him that nothing he could offer would be enough. Her voice, when it sounded, was so low he had to strain to hear it.

"You're wrong, Shane. You did reject me. Because this ability is part of who I am. Acceptance isn't a matter of degrees, it's a whole or nothing proposition. And you'll never be able to accept me for what I am."

The silence stretched between them, as dark and full as the night. He couldn't refute her words, and he couldn't give her the ones she wanted to hear. So in the end, he said nothing. Eventually he knew she slept. The tension seeped from her body and the exhaustion he suspected she was feeling overtook her completely.

But he remained awake for a long time, staring out in the darkness with thoughts as black as the shadows that surrounded them. And he had the notion, before sleep finally pulled him under, that life offered a man his share of regrets. If there was any shred of justice, Cassie wouldn't be one of his.

"Well, it took a lot of fast talking, but our charter will be here at first light." Liam Brooks slipped his cell phone into his shirt pocket and strolled back to the kitchen. He waited, then drawled, "What? No snarls about how long it's taken? No railing against the tornado gods or incompetent road crews?"

Hawk looked up slowly, closing the file in front of him. He saw the exact moment that Brooks realized what he'd been reading, thanks to the black expression that descended over his face.

"FBI files are classified, Donovan." With a few swift steps Liam was beside him, sweeping the file away. "Civilians don't have clearance."

Hawk noted the quiet anger in the man's voice. But he didn't regret his actions. He'd had to know the full extent of the danger Cassie was facing. And now that he did, it felt as if his heart was being squeezed in concrete vises.

"If she's caught…" It was difficult to get the words out. He tried again. "If Sheridan manages to inject her…she may as well be dead."

Some of the anger faded from Liam's face. "Imagining the worst-case scenario isn't going to help anything."

Swallowing hard, Hawk nodded toward the file in the agent's hand. "I read it in there, about the drug, I mean. Instant addiction? Total mind control? Pretty freaky stuff."

Brooks hesitated, then nodded. "Benedict has been perfecting this for a long time. He's a megalomaniac, but a bloody genius. And he has lots of experience in and around labs, creating his own designer drugs."

As much of that experience, Hawk thought sickly, came from the man's failures as from his successes. The file had detailed graphically the deaths of some of his other victims, as Benedict had perfected his trade. Some had even chosen death, rather than to live with the agony of the drug's influence.

And the thought of Cassie being faced with that kind of threat was going to be a constant, gnawing fear.

"Your sister's in her own territory. It's Sheridan who will be out of her element," Liam reminded him.

"It's doubtful she's alone, though."

"She's posed as a married couple with hired muscle before," the other man conceded. "She probably picked up another lackey. But just because we don't know Sheridan's or Cassie's whereabouts, doesn't mean Cassie isn't somewhere safe.''

Hawk rose, stalked to the window. The weather was still stormy, one thunderstorm after another. But the tornadoes had ended. Most of the roads in the area were impassable. He didn't doubt that they'd have a struggle tomorrow getting as far as the airport.

''I'd just feel better if the sheriff had found something at the ranch, you know? At least something that would have given an indication of where she and Farhold had gone.'' He slid a sideways glance toward the open bathroom door. Sheryl was washing out some of their clothes. He didn't want to burden her with his overwhelming worry for his sister. But neither could he let go of it himself.

What the sheriff and deputies had reported from the ranch had done nothing to calm his fears. The house had been deserted, the electricity and phone lines cut. Cassie's cell phone had been found in pieces, which would explain why he hadn't been able to reach her on it.

But the most chilling discoveries had been in the living room. A bullet embedded in the entertainment center, some sort of container in the fireplace. From the smell the sheriff had described, Liam guessed it was some sort of gas canister. Which left Hawk to wonder if the gas had done its job. Had it harmed Cassie or the baby? Had it incapacitated her and allowed Sheridan to capture her?

Fists knotted tightly at his side, he wheeled, paced. She and Farhold had gotten out of the house, he knew that much. Jim had found two horses gone. He'd also reported fence line mowed down. Because Sheridan had gone in pursuit? How far could Cassie and Farhold have ridden before the vehicle would catch up with them? And where the hell had they gone?

His cell phone sounded then, and he pulled it out, answered it on the first ring. Immediately he recognized Jim Burnhardt's voice. "Any sign of Cassie yet?"

The hesitation in the foreman's voice sent new dread circling in Hawk's stomach. "No, but we've recovered the horses. One was lame. Both were saddled and had joined the herd in the north pasture. We're still searching, but we haven't found a sign of Cassie. I'm sorry, Hawk."

"Yeah." With effort, he tamped down the frustration surging through him. "Call the sheriff and let him know, would you?"

"The sheriff's here. On the ranch, I mean. And there are some agents here, too. They're combing the spread for any trace of Cassie and Dr. Farhold."

"Have they discovered anything?" Hawk couldn't prevent the flare of hope from sounding in his words.

"Not yet. But the sheriff is lining up some men to help in the search, so they can cover more ground."

"Okay, I'll be there tomorrow. But call if there are any developments."

Ending the call, he looked at Liam, saw the questions in his eyes. "The agents have arrived." He had to swallow before he could force the rest out. "The horses have been found, riderless."

"Times like these call for a little faith," Liam said quietly. "Faith in your sister and her friend. Give them some credit. Sounds like they've already given Sheridan a run for her money."

Hawk nodded slowly, unable to give voice to the dread that was curling in his belly. Faith was increasingly hard to summon. Somehow he'd have felt a whole lot better if those horses hadn't been discovered.

Chapter 9

"It's morning!" Cassie was aghast. Her eyes had opened to find the sky a soft gray, with only the barest hint of color above the treetops. But it signaled dawn's approach, and she would have sworn she'd slept for no more than a couple of hours.

A thread of panic unfurled. How many hours had they wasted? Had the kidnappers been able to follow in the darkness? If so, how much closer had they drawn by now? She tried to rise, found it impossible. A heavy weight across her legs, another around her torso, kept her trapped. She began to struggle before she looked down, and understanding filtered in.

Shane's arm was firmly around her waist, keeping her pressed closely to his body. One leg was thrown over both of hers, neatly pinning her in place. There was a seal of heat at her back, where he was pressed against her, and she wondered now how she'd missed that sensation upon waking. Sharing a bed with

Shane had always been like sleeping with a furnace, and the body heat they'd generated had more than warded off the night chill.

For a few moments she lay quietly, her initial panic dispelled. It was all too easy to lie here like this with him. To remember the times she'd woken in his arms, to find him looking down at her tenderly. He'd told her one time that he loved watching her sleep. The confession had disconcerted her at the time. But it occurred to her now that she'd never been the one free to observe him in slumber.

The temptation grew, too much to resist. With no little effort she squirmed around in his grasp until she faced him. At her movements a frown flickered across his face, his fingers clutched for her briefly before relaxing again. She lay quietly in his arms, barely daring to breathe, until he seemed to settle again.

His whiskers shadowed his jawline and gave him a disreputable look that didn't mesh with his usual professional demeanor. Cassie tried to remember if she'd ever seen him with more than a five-o'clock shadow, and realized she hadn't. With the casual clothes, rifle and the beginnings of a beard, he looked like a throwback to the stars of those TV westerns. A smile tilted her lips, but quickly faded as she puzzled over the change in him. Because it was more than surface.

She hadn't forgotten the easy way he'd handled the rifle the time he'd taken it out of their gun cabinet. Or the bullet he'd put through the window when it had become all too clear that someone was trying to get in the side door. She hadn't had to explain how to load the firearm or how to carry it safely. So where had this unexplained familiarity come from?

Answers weren't forthcoming. His chest continued to rise and fall peacefully; his thick, short brush of lashes remained closed. Cassie watched him, feeling her heart expand dangerously. She'd always wondered if his dark brown hair would curl like this if he let it grow a bit. The whiskers blurred the square chin, but the stubbornness it hinted at was amply demonstrated in his personality. There was determination evident in the firm line of his lips, compassion in his more sensitive brow. She thought both were necessary in his line of work.

Her gaze traveled to the scar then, and obeying an unconscious compulsion, she traced the jagged pink line that twisted from beneath his chin down across his throat. It was slightly raised to the touch, and she wondered if it was difficult to shave around. Did it still hurt him? How was it that she could have seen the danger that surrounded his getting shot, and not the threat that resulted in this injury?

It was useless to question the ability she'd been born with. It defied prediction. It just appeared at random intervals and left her to interpret what the dreams meant.

And now, of course, the visions, as well.

As her finger traced down his throat, her hand was caught in one of his, surprising her. A moment later, his eyes opened, staring directly into hers. Their deep brown was almost the same color as his hair and at one time she'd thought they could see through her, clear to her soul.

She'd been wrong.

"What happened?" Her fingertip still rested on the scar, making further words unnecessary.

It took him a moment to respond and when he did, his voice was still gravelly with sleep. "Knife."

Little needles of shock darted through her. "I'm guessing you didn't slip during surgery."

Shane released a breath, unable to look away from her. "No. I didn't slip." He was usually more adept at keeping these particular memories locked away. They preyed most often at night when sleep lowered his defenses. And with the remnants of slumber still too close, they crept in easily, like thieves in the dark.

"The hospital I worked at for the first two weeks was in Kabul. But after that I volunteered to go to one of the more mobile clinics that serve the villages in the southern portion of the country. Most of the people there are unable to get to the city for medical attention and the need was high."

He stopped. It was too easy to see all the faces, a mental mural of suffering humanity that had met them at each stop. The days had been long, as an endless stream of villagers would pour in. The most routine complaints had gone untreated for so long they'd developed into far more serious problems. One stop began to blur with another after a while. The constant had always been the unnecessary deaths. Pneumonia because of a lack of available antibiotics, scurvy from a shortage of vitamin C, and an outbreak of cholera that resulted from contaminated drinking water. It was a death count difficult to imagine after practicing medicine in the States.

"A couple weeks passed before I elected to stay at one of the more stationary units where the most serious cases were brought. They needed surgeons there, and we did some good. The biggest obstacle, though, was our supplies constantly being hijacked.''

Keeping Cassie's hand in his, he rested them on his chest. With his thumb skating across her knuckles, he continued. "Our supply line came out of Sharan, in the southeast portion of the country, but half the time the drivers never made it back with the food and medicines. Drugs, especially, had become a high value commodity in the area, and with various warlords fighting for power in the area, the drugs were sold on the black market to help pay for political favors.''

"They stole the food and medicine meant to help their own people?'' There was a mixture of shock and indignation in Cassie's voice.

"The region is fiercely tribal, with fractured loyalties. The drugs paid for food and necessities for the thieves. I doubt they considered the moral niceties. Sometimes we'd have a couple U.S. or British soldiers around to help secure the delivery. Other times we had to arm ourselves and take our chances.''

He could still remember the first time he'd taken his turn doing so. The stories he'd heard of the ambushed drivers had rung all too clearly in his mind. The lucky ones made it back to camp with no more than a few bruises and broken bones. The less fortunate were left for dead.

And the damned were taken hostage.

"That wasn't the job of a bunch of doctors, for heaven's sake!'' Cassie's voice shook with emotion. "If the government couldn't see to your safety, you had no business being there at all.''

One corner of his mouth pulled upward in a humorless smile. "It's hard to think that way when you have people dying all around you. They didn't choose to live that way. The danger wasn't their doing. They were *people,* same as you and me. With homes, families. We wanted to do what we could for them."

Her fingers squeezed his. "So you went for supplies."

"It was my third trip." Memories crowded in, and for a moment he could almost feel the searing heat. Taste the dust kicked up by their jeep. "They caught us at dusk. We'd made the transfer from the Sharan truck and were bringing it back to the camp." That stretch had always been the most dangerous, he recalled. Once they'd parted from the more heavily armed truck, they'd headed back with only two or three armed personnel. There had never been room to carry many people; they'd needed the space for the boxes of supplies. "A group of thieves caught us forty miles out. The driver was killed outright." His name was Robert Ludlow, Shane recalled, and he'd been a general practitioner from Arkansas. He was a new grandpa and never tired of showing pictures of his daughter's son.

"The other doctor and I were taken hostage. From what we were able to piece together later, the local warlord would hold captives for ransom. He'd try to sell them back to their government, or to their families. We were taken to a camp of sorts and kept tied up in a tent for ten days or so." He'd never been exactly certain how long. "There were others there, nine or ten of us in all."

He had to stop then, suddenly swamped by emotion so powerful it stole his breath. Once the captives had started dying, the closed quarters of the tent had kept the odor of death surrounding them, until Shane had been able to smell it on himself, in his pores and his hair, as well as on the other survivors.

"I'm not sure what happened. We could tell by our captor's tempers that things weren't going well. Maybe the ransom demands weren't being answered. But they finally decided they couldn't afford to share even what little food they did with us. So they started pulling captives out of the tent and killing them."

They didn't waste bullets on them, Shane recalled bitterly. Ammunition was much too precious to be spent unwisely. A couple of others had been beaten to death. Most had had their throats cut. Each time the body would be dragged back to the tent, thrown inside.

"By the last day there were three of us left. A man came to the tent, pulled me out of it." And he'd known, been certain, that he would be the next to die. His hands had already been tied behind his back. He'd been forced to his knees, head pulled back by the hair, so his eyes were blinded by the sun blazing overhead. There had been the sound of voices around him, laughter. And then his vision had been filled with his killer's face.

The man had said something taunting in his language, smiled and raised the knife. The sunshine had caught the shiny blade, reflected off it in dazzling brilliance. Distantly, he'd been aware of the sound of approaching vehicles, excited shouts. But his focus was on the tip of the knife, pressing under his chin, then through the skin. There had been agonizing pain, then, miraculously, that knife was gone, and so was his persecutor.

''The warlord had sent word that he had a use for us after all. Apparently he was trying to curry favor with the new foreign government and those of us still alive were delivered as a good faith offering.'' And if one of the other captors hadn't run up to grab his would-be killer's hand, his body would be broiling right now in the Afghan desert.

''You should have come home then.'' Somehow the anger in Cassie's voice was easier to deal with than pity or horror. ''They should have insisted you return. Instead you stayed…how much longer?''

''I signed up for another month.'' He couldn't explain to her why he'd done so. His reasons had been in such a tangled mess he'd been unable to identify all of them himself. He had been certain that if he left, the killers would win. He'd been unwilling to concede them that.

''The scar makes the injury look worse than it was. Once we were delivered back to Kabul, I was stitched up and had no further problems with the wound. I returned to the clinic I'd been working at before it all happened.'' He blinked, watching the pink and orange hues bleed across the sky as the sun rose. The forested wilderness couldn't have been farther removed from the mountains and searing deserts where he'd served for three months. But the danger was the same.

''And the gunshot wound?'' Cassie raised her head, looked into his eyes. ''When did that happen?''

A door inside him abruptly slammed shut. ''We need to get moving.''

''Shane.'' Her gaze was searching and much too hard to meet as he put her away from him and rolled to his feet.

"You never thought you'd sleep all night, did you?" His tone sounded false, even to his own ears. He busied himself shaking out the blankets as Cassie rose and stepped aside. "What do you say we go over and check out those raspberry bushes I spotted last night? You might make a survivalist out of me yet."

Cassie helped him roll up the blankets and secured them to their packs. It was as if a curtain had been dropped, she thought, suddenly and completely, keeping all of his emotions trapped inside. Keeping her out.

And it was ridiculous to resent the ease with which he managed it. She'd wondered what had caused the changes in them and now she knew. He'd nearly died. Her fingers faltered. Although the scene of him being shot had played in her mind over and over, she'd never imagined him enduring this sort of horror, as well. What kind of psychic ability was it that would warn of one risk and not the other? What use was it, really, when it failed to help her prevent the worst from happening?

Straightening her clothing, she rose, fell in silently behind him as he strode toward the bushes in question. She knew well the futility of railing against that which couldn't be explained. That which couldn't be changed. And she also realized that had she dreamed of the scene he'd described, she would have been unsuccessful at dissuading him from going anyway.

The problem didn't stem from her inability to warn him. It came from his refusal to believe her. To trust her, just enough to let his heart overrule his head.

Her mood morose, she fell in step slightly behind him. He reached the clump of bushes before she did, and had already plucked off a handful. "Definitely not raspberries. They look more like wild grapes."

"Don't eat those," she said sharply, once she saw what he had in his cupped palm. For good measure, she upset his hand, sending the collected berries to the ground below. "That's moonseed, and the berries are poisonous. They can even be fatal if ingested."

Shane looked at the spilled berries, then at her. "I wasn't going to eat them, at least not until you okayed it. I'm not that green."

She raised her brows. "You looked ready and willing to me."

Grimacing, he said, "Maybe it was the visions of fresh fruit in my head. Raspberry jam on a toasted bagel."

Cassie almost groaned at the thought. "Waffles with strawberries and whipped cream."

"Scrambled eggs with ham and peppers."

"Silver dollar pancakes with maple syrup." They fell in step together, each of them trying to outdo the other by conjuring up a breakfast feast mirage.

"French toast dusted with powdered sugar and smoked bacon."

"Steak and eggs, a Texas favorite," Shane shot back.

Cassie held her stomach. "French pastries, you know, the kind with the fruit filling and the really flaky crusts. And a chocolate mocha cappuccino."

Shane cocked his head. "I seem to recall a time you ate almost all of that at one sitting." He was wise enough to dodge the elbow she jabbed at him.

"Now who's the comedian? You've always ex-aggerated my appetite."

"I've seen lumberjacks eat less," he declared solemnly, kicking one booted foot free of the saw briar twining around it. "Football players. Sumo wrestlers."

She slanted him a sidelong glance. "Are you saying I'm fat?"

"Not at all. Just that your metabolism is a medical miracle."

"Nice save, Dr. Farhold." Shifting her stick to the crook of her arm, she held up her hand to shield her eyes. "Keep being nice to me and I'll find us some raspberry bushes yet. The wildlife has probably already gotten to them, though. I'm not sure how good any remaining berries would be by this time of the year."

But a couple hours later she was probably even more surprised than Shane when they actually happened on a thicket of raspberry bushes. Most of the branches had been stripped clean. Only the brave or the very desperate would attempt to reach the berries left on the inside branches, entwined as they were with thorned vines.

"This looks like an excellent place for a picnic," Shane declared. With undisguised eagerness he slipped off his pack and set down his rifle.

"It's going to take some work to get them," Cassie noted. "I think I'll leave you to it while I answer nature's call."

Shane narrowed his gaze suspiciously. "You can't possibly have to go again. You just went an hour ago."

She smiled innocently. "You know pregnant women and their bladders."

"Yeah, yeah," she heard him mutter as she made her way around to the other side of the thicket. "I

know something about lazy women, too. And I recognize when I'm being snowed into doing the
work.''

''What was that?'' she called, biting her lip to
keep from laughing. ''I didn't catch all of it.''

''Nothing, nothing. Hey, these aren't bad. A little
sour, but beggars can't be choosers.''

The unmistakable sound of smacking lips had her
hurrying in her task and shortly heading back toward
him. ''No fair, you're supposed to save some for
me.'' She rounded the clump of bushes. ''At least
wait until there's a whole pile before you—''

The ground rocked beneath her feet. The sky
dulled as her vision hazed. A fireworks display of
color burst from beneath her eyelids, and she felt as
if she was being hurled through space at Mach 1
speed. She wasn't aware of the whimper that escaped
her lips. Sight and hearing shut down as her senses
turned inward.

''That's right, cry.'' Shane reached in between
several branches with particularly wicked-looking
thorns to free some plump berries. ''Because I'm
making the rules. If you don't pick, you don't eat.
It's called tough love, baby.'' Carefully, he set the
berries he'd plucked onto the small pile he'd started
atop his pack.

He picked several more before stopping to listen.
''Cass? I'm not doing this all myself. I've already
been wounded.'' When there was no answer, concern
formed. ''Cass?'' He started around the thicket, and
stopped short when he saw her standing a few feet
away. With a muttered curse he raced over to her.
She'd gone completely still. Her gaze was fixed, staring, and when he came to a stop in front of her he

had the eerie sensation that she was looking right through him.

Panic jackhammered in his chest, and his reaction was instinctive. "It's okay, baby, it's okay. I've got you." With one fluid movement he slipped an arm around her waist and lowered her to the ground. Unwilling to leave her side, he knelt over her, smoothed his hand along her jaw while crooning to her, as if he could bring her back with the physical reminders of his presence.

Time crawled, but it was probably only moments later she blinked and looked around, her expression confused. A wave of relief jolted through him as he noted that her eyes, while clouded, were focused. "God, Cassie, you scared me to death." What happened when she underwent one of these episodes while she was alone? The thought sent darts of terror firing through his veins. She could have one working with the horses. While driving. Hell, she could step out in front of a car in Greenlaurel. No wonder Hawk had gone tearing off to North Carolina to find a way to help her. The frequency with which they were occurring was frightening.

She struggled in his arms, although her movements were weak. "Hafta go."

Her speech was slightly slurred. Checking her pulse, he found it pounding. Shane wasn't sure how long the episode had lasted. Probably not as long as it had seemed, but it had felt interminable. A wave of helplessness crashed over him, as infuriating as it was unfamiliar. There was nothing he could do for her out here. And according to Cassie, nothing the doctors at Greenlaurel Community Hospital had been able to do for her, either.

"We have to go. Now." Her voice was stronger now, and so was she.

"It's not going to hurt anything to rest a little bit."

But he couldn't keep her down for more than a couple seconds before she managed to struggle to her feet. "There's no time."

She grabbed her pack, and he resigned himself to the inevitable. There was no use having her get more agitated. "Okay. Just let me get my things."

"Hurry." She started walking away at a far swifter pace than he would have thought she was capable of. He scooped up the berries and poured them into his coat pocket. Then he picked up his things and took off after her.

Jogging to catch up, he snagged the back of her coat. "Hey. What's your hurry?"

She looked over her shoulder at him. "C'mon." She appeared fully recovered, he observed with relief. Slowing, he came to a halt. Tucking one hand in his pocket, he brought out a berry, held it up tantalizingly. "Look what I've got." If she showed signs of an appetite, it would relieve a fraction of the worry still weighing on him.

"Being the kind, generous soul that I am, I just might be prevailed upon to share them with you. If you ask really really nicely."

But she wasn't looking at him anymore. She was staring over his shoulder, a shudder racking her. "Guess you're not the only one craving fresh fruit this morning."

Following the direction of her gaze, Shane felt his breathing strangle in his lungs. There, in approximately the same place he'd been risking his skin for wild raspberries, was a huge brown bear, sticking one paw into the center of the bush with a great deal less care than he had. Within a few feet were three cubs, tumbling about in the grass.

"Good Lord, would you look at the size of those paws?" he said in awe.

"It's probably a good idea to keep moving," Cassie reminded him. "I'd be more comfortable putting more distance between us."

Because her idea had merit, he continued walking, head craned to look behind him. "I didn't know there were bears around here."

"There are more than there used to be, thanks to conservation efforts. Was there a tag on the adult's ear? That would mean it was part of a study the state is conducting to monitor the bear population."

"I think I'll pass on getting close enough to look for a tag," he said dryly, throwing a last glance at the animal. The bear was sitting on its haunches now, enjoying, quite literally, the fruits of its labors. One of the cubs had approached, no doubt looking for a handout. "You know if we hadn't left when we did, things could have gotten ugly...." Shane's voice trailed off as comprehension slammed into him.

Reaching out, he grabbed hold of Cassie's coat, pulled her around to face him. "Back there you had one of your spells again..."

"I knew the bear was coming," she affirmed simply, her gaze steady. "I didn't see it. Not the way you're thinking. But I knew it, all the same."

"That's not possible." His denial sounded automatic, but it was exactly what she'd expected to hear. Which didn't explain the wave of desolation that washed over her.

"Now, why did I know you would say that?" She

smiled mockingly, then turned away again. "And by the way, you're welcome. I'm told bear maulings can be a trifle unpleasant."

His silence had a grim little smile crossing her lips. She could almost hear the wheels turning in that all too logical mind of his. They walked awhile longer before he said finally, "You said that these episodes are getting more frequent."

"Yes," she admitted. And they were bound to get more so the longer she went without the tea. "But they aren't anything to worry about." She didn't think it wise to mention the times they'd happened when she was working with the horses. Hawk had been a great deal more concerned when she'd narrowly avoided being trampled during one of the spells. But right now they had a far more serious danger to deal with.

"I'll worry until we find something that controls them."

She whirled on him then, suddenly sick of covering the same territory with him. "I told you, I have something, and it works quite well. Once we get back to the ranch—" Her voice faltered here, before she steadied it. "I can start drinking the tea again and things will be fine."

He'd stopped, too, and was surveying her soberly. "Have you considered the fact that these spells began at approximately the same time you became pregnant?"

She nodded impatiently. "I told you that. Originally that's how I discovered I was pregnant. We were running all these other tests."

"You also said the episodes are getting stronger as the pregnancy progresses."

Stronger and clearer, she thought. The first ones she'd had included only the symptoms, and a hazy, almost dreamlike feeling. But with each passing week, they had solidified, until she was seeing scenes, like the one with the bears, with color and sound and detail.

But then his words echoed in her mind, sparking another nebulous idea. *The episodes are getting stronger as the pregnancy progresses.*

She stared at him wordlessly, her thoughts whirling madly. Hawk had discovered their mother had suffered these same types of spells while she'd been pregnant with them. What would have caused such similar experiences between her and her birth mother? Like smoke in the wind, the words of the fair's fortune-teller came back to her.

Your daughter will share your gift and you will teach her to use it well....

"I know you've probably had your fill of tests, but it wouldn't hurt to take you to the University of Texas Health Science Center at Houston for a second opinion. This is serious, Cass."

"It's the baby," she whispered, staring at him blankly. Certainty reared. She didn't know how she knew it, but she did.

"I know, honey," Shane's voice was gentle. "And we'll get to the bottom of this, one way or another. I'm not going to let anything happen to you, or to the baby."

She shook her head impatiently. He wouldn't understand. He'd never understand. The sorrow that filled her then was as much for their unborn child as it was for her. "I told you that Hawk found files indicating that we were triplets, not twins. I haven't met my other brother, Dare, so I can't speak for him, but Hawk has always had an inexplicable communication with animals.'' She shook her head, trying to make sense of it all. ''What if my birth mother suffered these episodes because she was carrying three children with psychic ability?''

His expression was deliberately blank. ''Why would you think that?''

''Remember the fortune-teller at the fair?'' She could tell by the sudden tightening in his jaw that he did. ''She foretold all of this. You being hurt in Afghanistan, me being pregnant with a daughter—one who shared my gifts…'' Without thinking she reached out to grip his arm. ''Maybe the episodes are getting stronger as the baby develops. And maybe this new manifestation of precognition isn't stemming from me at all. These flashes into the future might be coming from our baby.''

Shane worked his shoulders uneasily, deliberately averting his gaze. ''Cass, c'mon. You can't believe that.''

But she did. The pieces had clicked into place. The stranger at the fair had predicted it. Cassie herself had experienced it.

And the baby's father would never believe it.

''What will you do if it's true, Shane?'' she asked achingly. ''You walked away from me rather than try to accept something you couldn't understand. If our baby is psychic, will you reject her, too?''

Chapter 10

Hours later, they'd covered a great deal more territory by foot. But they were no closer to a meeting of the minds. Shane was still mulling her words. *Will you reject her, too?*

The intervening time hadn't lessened their sting. He'd been angered by Cassie's suggestion. Hurt. How many times had he already assured her that he'd be there for the baby? What would it take to convince her? He'd spent much of his childhood grappling with the secret fear that his father had left them because of him. If only he'd been better behaved. Smarter. More athletic. As an adult he'd come to realize that his father's desertion was due to a weakness in the man, not the child. But the years of doubt had been devastating.

If our baby is psychic…

His mouth flattened. Cassie was convinced she possessed an ability that was widely disproven. The province of fakes and charlatans, gullible fools and wise cons. But he'd never persuade her she was wrong. He'd come to recognize that. There wasn't enough research he could show her, enough experts and studies he could quote that would sway her.

And now she was suggesting the baby possessed psychic ability as well.

His nape prickled as he thought once again of the mother bear that had arrived at the raspberry bushes only minutes after Cassie had urged him out of there. He wasn't fooled by the picture it had made with her frolicking cubs. He knew just enough about wildlife to understand bears were aggressively protective of their young. He didn't want to think about what might have happened if they hadn't left exactly when they had.

He thought back, trying to picture Cassie's position when she'd had her last spell.

He hadn't noticed the approaching bears, and the bushes would have blocked them from her sight, as well. Nor had he heard anything that would have alerted him to their presence. A sliver of unease pricked at him. If she hadn't seen or heard the animals, how could she have known they were coming?

People had hunches, of course, a sort of intuition that was probably derived from the subconscious picking up on details that the conscious mind had missed. But the frequency and timing of hers were nothing short of uncanny.

First there had been the shot fired through the window. He'd thought that perhaps she'd seen the moonlight glinting off a gun barrel. But recalling it now, he remembered that the gun the man had pointed at them hadn't been a long-barreled rifle, but an automatic pistol with a dull black silencer attached.

Then there had been the snake. Just the memory had sweat beading on his forehead. Neither of them could have seen the thing, positioned as it was on the ledge beneath them. Cassie had come out of the spell muttering warnings about it, so it wasn't likely she'd heard its warning rattle minutes before it had struck at him.

There had to be another explanation for these glimpses into the future. No one's intuition was that good. Or that convenient.

That idea triggered a memory of some of the scientific theories being proposed to account for a flood of reported near-death experiences. One, he recalled, suggested the scenes were induced by lack of oxygen, and yet another hypothesized that they were caused by stimulation to the temporal lobe of the brain in times of great stress or danger. Perhaps research on neurotransmitter receptors, still in its infancy, would shed light on what Cassie was going through.

But for the first time the idea of a logical answer failed to soothe as it normally did. Doubt was chipping away at years of scientific certainty. Shane was beginning to believe that no amount of tests would be enough to adequately explain what she was experiencing.

And if science couldn't supply the answer, that left him with only one to consider—the one Cassie believed herself.

By late afternoon Cassie's shoulders were drooping despite the more frequent breaks Shane had insisted on. Even with fatigue evident, however, she seemed more eager than ever to push on. Finally she said, "The cabin is around here somewhere. I recognize the area." She pointed to where a herd of white-tailed deer were collected about a hundred yards away. "They're drinking from the same stream that runs in back of the cabin. Farther north it gets rockier, and the slopes get steeper. The water's deeper there, too. On the other side of it will be the cabin."

She threw him a bright smile, hope and relief evident in it. "Hawk might already be there. Once he figures out that we headed to the forest, it won't take him long to guess our destination."

He nodded, not wanting to spoil her mood. But he knew they needed to be prepared for the cabin to be empty. If Hawk wasn't there with help, if the kidnappers had managed to follow them, then they were not much better off than they'd been at the ranch.

Cassie was walking with renewed purpose, despite the fact that her energy had been visibly flagging earlier. He'd cut out his tongue before mentioning his fears to her. But his mind was already busily planning. He had to be prepared to hold off the kidnappers from the cabin alone, if need be. Because despite their head start, despite the fact that they hadn't seen a sign of the couple since they'd entered the forest, he didn't underestimate Sheridan's resolve to snatch Cassie.

It couldn't begin to match his determination to keep her safe.

It was another hour before the cabin came into sight, and he had to stop Cassie when she would have approached it. "Let's just watch it for a while, for any signs of life."

She frowned. "I don't see any possible way Sheridan and her sidekick could have reached here first if they were trailing us."

"Maybe not. But don't forget the drugmakers we came upon. We don't know who else might have taken up residence in there. So we'll watch for a while."

Because his words made sense, Cassie curbed her impatience and nodded. She squatted beside him, prepared to keep vigil. And as the minutes turned into an hour, excitement shriveled into disappointment. "I think it's empty," she said.

Shane sent her a quick glance. "It looks like it. Above the door there's a bird's nest that looks occupied. It's unlikely the bird would still be there if the door was being used."

She would have commented on his increased knowledge of the outdoors, but she was too busy grappling with blossoming disillusionment. She didn't know what could have kept Hawk, but she'd expected him to reach this place long before they did. Was it possible that he hadn't considered they'd head for the cabin? That he'd forgotten the way? Neither scenario seemed likely. She drew a deep breath, then released it in a rush. Right now they had little choice but to wait for him to bring help.

She just hoped it arrived before the kidnappers did.

The key to the cabin was still on a hook outside the front door. It had been there as long as Cassie could remember. She didn't know who had built the structure, or how long ago. But it was used by anyone needing to take shelter from the wild, hunters or campers alike.

It was a bit more run-down than she'd remembered

it. The hinges screeched loudly when Shane opened the door, and the jamb sagged on one side. She had the thought that it wouldn't take more than one or two strong kicks to break it down, then firmly shoved the notion away.

Tearing aside a monstrous cobweb, she walked inside, took inventory. Other than appearing a bit more dilapidated, it looked much like it had two years ago, the last time she'd been here.

"Home sweet home."

"It's not much. My dad used to do some repairs on it every time we came up here, but he's been dead three years. I'd bet nothing has been done to it since." She roamed around the inside, poking about. "Someone's been here since the last time I came, though." She nodded toward a few dusty cans of spaghetti sitting on a narrow set of shelves beside one window. "I didn't leave those."

Shane was squinting up at the beamed ceiling. "The roof still looks solid, although I guess we won't really know unless it rains. And the windows are unbroken. We might just get lucky and not have any four-legged friends as company tonight."

Cassie surveyed the rest of the interior. Everything else was much as she'd left it the last time she'd camped here. There was a set of double cupboards on one wall, with a narrow table beneath that passed for a counter. Crossing to open the cupboard, she spied the portable cookstove inside. "Hey, maybe we could actually have hot food tonight. At least if there's any gas still left in it." She examined it further. "Empty. Guess we'll feast on summer sausage again." The other shelves held nothing but a few odds and ends. Fishing line, a few lures and some tattered copies of the murder mysteries her dad used to favor.

"If you have a can opener, we can always try the spaghetti." Shane picked up one of the cans to peer at it. "It's not too far past the expiration date."

"It might come to that."

The rest of the furnishings were spartan—a plain wooden table with four chairs, and a bed shoved into one corner with a bare mattress. There was little here that would be a temptation to thieves, which was probably why it remained untampered with.

The cabin needed a thorough cleaning before she was willing to spend time in it. She set her pack down and went to get the broom. When she turned back toward the room, however, Shane had his pack down as well and was rummaging inside it.

"What are you looking for?"

He didn't look up. "The pocket knife."

Her brows rose. "You weren't kidding about the spaghetti, huh?"

He retrieved the knife and looked at her. "First things first. We don't have much daylight left. I want to rig up some sort of perimeter defense that will warn us if someone gets near, maybe slow them down at the same time."

"Like a booby trap?"

He grinned—a quick flash of teeth. "Something along those lines, yeah."

She nodded, trying to hide the unease skittering down her spine. She knew what his precautions meant. They weren't running anymore—they were making a stand. And because they were no longer on the move, it wasn't a matter of *if* Sheridan would catch up with them—it was *when*.

Shane's face had sobered. He was watching her carefully, as if for any show of fear on her part. But strangely enough, she wasn't scared. Not now, anyway. And that fact was due in no little part to the man standing before her.

"Tell me what to do," she said simply, heading for the door. "I'll help."

Even by plane the trip back to the ranch had seemed endless. Jim had been waiting at the airport, but when he'd admitted there was nothing new to report, Hawk's spirits had sunk even lower.

Now, standing in the living room of the ranch, staring at the bullet hole in the entertainment center, he felt his blood turn to ice. He wasn't aware of Sheryl coming up beside him until she slipped her hand into his and squeezed hard. "There's no indication that anyone was hurt," she reminded him quietly.

No, there was no blood. Other than the damage the bullet had done, there was little indication of what had gone on here after his last phone call to Cassie. The canister the sheriff had reported discovering had been sent away to have its contents tested. He looked at Frank Lloyd, the county sheriff. "Farhold's place in town has been checked?"

The man pushed away from the wall he was leaning against. In his thirties, he was a relatively young man for the position, in an area where the people tended to vote for experience. But he'd always impressed Hawk with his solid investigative skills. "The doctor hasn't been seen since he picked up some prescriptions a couple days ago."

"How about that place he and Cassie had gone to

a few months ago?'' He hadn't been able to come up with a name for the bed-and-breakfast his sister had stayed at, but he'd told Frank the name of the town.

The sheriff shook his head. ''They haven't been back since that one visit. I've checked with all the neighbors. Not one of them has seen Cassie.'' He paused before adding reluctantly, ''Tucker Vance thought he heard shots, though, that night you first called me.''

''Was there anywhere special on the ranch that you and Cassie used to go?'' Sheryl asked Hawk. ''Maybe somewhere she could have gone to hide?''

''I've tried to think, but I can't come up with anything other than what I told Frank before.''

''We looked in the basement, and that door was opened from the inside. So it looks as though they might have left the house that way.''

''It's how we used to sneak out when we didn't want to risk waking our parents,'' Hawk said, his throat suddenly full. ''We always went to that outcrop of rock in the north pasture.''

''Checked that, too,'' Frank said quietly. ''Nothing. This ranch is pretty big, though. We haven't covered it all. We'll come up with something.''

Hawk didn't voice the truth floating unspoken between them. What chance did Cassie and Farhold have on foot when the kidnappers had a vehicle? The answer was chillingly obvious.

The sheriff's portable radio crackled, and he unclipped it from his belt to answer it. A moment later he looked out at the group, a grim expression on his face. ''One of the deputies has found a truck hidden in some brush about a mile south of the timberline. It's a rental.''

''The timberline?'' Hawk murmured. Unthinkingly he slipped his arm around Sheryl's waist to bring her close as if for fortification.

''There's nothing in it to indicate who was driving it. But the deputy gave a description of the woman we're looking for to the clerk at the rental place and it rang a bell. She's traveling with a man.''

''Sheridan,'' Liam breathed.

''I don't understand.'' Sheryl tipped her face up to Hawk's, frowning. ''What's it mean? Your sister is on foot and so are the people chasing her?''

''She led them into the forest.'' Hawk exchanged a grim look with Liam. ''If Cassie made it that close to the timberline, it's the first place she'd head. She's familiar with it. We both are.''

Brooks whistled. ''She's a gutsy one. Not a bad idea, all things considered. How large an area are we talking here?''

''Huge, but it doesn't matter.'' Excitement mounted. He was on the right track finally. He could feel it. ''I know where she'd go. There's a small cabin in the forest. My family used to camp there when I was a kid. I haven't been there in six or seven years, but Cassie sometimes goes up there.''

''How long to get there?''

''It's a full day ride by horseback.'' Hawk looked out the window at the late-afternoon sun as he answered the agent's question, felt his momentary excitement sink right along with it.

''Horseback?'' Liam sounded dismayed. ''There's no other way? How about chopper?''

''Not in those woods.'' The sheriff shook his head.

"You go by foot, or on well-traveled trails by horse." Frank looked at Hawk. "You know we'll have to wait until first light," he said quietly.

He didn't say anything. He couldn't. His throat was seized by frustration and despair. Logically, he knew the man was right. By nightfall they would barely have started the trip. Taking horses on that trail at night was out of the question. It would be much too grueling for the animals in the dark. And it had been so long since he'd been to the cabin, he doubted his ability to find it without light to find familiar landmarks.

Sheryl stroked his arm. "Cassie was smart enough to think of a perfect place to hide. She'll outsmart Sheridan, too. We'll wait until first light and then ride out."

He pulled her closer, rested his chin on her hair. "Not a chance. You're staying here." Despite her protests, he remained unmoved. He wasn't about to risk the woman he loved. He was already in hell having his sister in unimaginable danger.

Cassie hadn't asked questions. Not at first. She'd accompanied Shane outside and gathered as many stout sticks as she could find. But when she dumped the first armload in front of him and he picked one up, began whittling an end, she couldn't help herself. "Making us a supply of spears? Maybe we could use them down at the brook to catch some fish. Do you like sushi?"

"Let's just say, it's well outranked by summer sausage, which I doubt I will ever be able to look at again." He held up a stick that he'd already sharpened into a point. "One end will go into the ground and the other will be a nasty little surprise for anyone who trips over it.''

She was impressed, in spite of herself. ''Something you picked up in Boy Scouts?''

He'd already returned to his whittling. ''No, in Afghanistan.''

Sobered by his answer, she went back to collecting more sticks. She still hadn't come to terms with the horrors that he'd suffered over there. Still didn't understand why he hadn't come home while he'd had the chance.

And he still hadn't told her about how he'd been shot.

Cassie shuddered. She couldn't imagine anything worse than what he'd already revealed. An ordeal like that couldn't help but change a man. And he hadn't had much time to recover, physically or emotionally before he'd come to the ranch and become embroiled in even more conflict. First finding out he was going to be a father, then being shot at and going on the run.

If it hadn't been for her note he'd still be safely back in Greenlaurel, not fending off crazed pursuers. But there hadn't been a moment in this entire situation when he'd made her feel as if he regretted being by her side in this.

All his regrets seemed reserved for what could never be resolved between them.

When she dropped another load of sticks at his feet, he looked up and said, ''Take the ones I've finished and poke them in the ground beside those. See how I've started?'' She nodded and went about the task. He'd sharpened both ends, so they were easier to push into the ground. She continued the random pattern he'd begun, in concentric circles surrounding the cabin. An unsuspecting intruder would have to have excellent night vision to avoid tripping and falling over one and having another rammed into his midsection.

Once she finished, she saw that he'd gone through the debris out back for some ancient tin cans. Fascinated, she watched him pour into each some pebbles he'd collected, then tape down the lids with adhesive tape from the first-aid kit. He used the knife to punch holes through the sides, then threaded fishing line through the can.

She marveled at his ingenuity. "I take it these are our noisemakers."

"As good as an alarm," he affirmed. When he finished she helped him weave the line with the cans around the sticks on the outer perimeter.

When they'd finished, they used the dwindling sunlight to give the cabin a quick cleaning. And when that task was done, Cassie coaxed him into allowing her to go down to the brook to wash up. He'd finally given in, perhaps realizing that this wasn't an argument he could win. He'd kept watch while she'd found the deepest part of the water for the closest thing to a bath she'd had since leaving the ranch. The water was chilly enough to keep her from lingering. After changing into clean clothes, she'd washed her hair, too. Then, shivering but feeling decidedly more fresh, she'd stood guard while Shane did the same.

Feeling clean had improved her mood to the point that she almost didn't mind summer sausage and apples again for supper. Almost. When they got back to the cabin Cassie took out a flashlight and set it on the table, its beam pointed at the door, so Shane could see to lock it.

She slipped off her coat and hung it over the back of one of the chairs. He dragged one of them over to wedge it beneath the knob. Then he stood looking at the windows.

Reading his thoughts, she said, "We could tape rags over them."

"Good idea."

She fetched the rags and held one up at each window so he could tape the top to the window frame, leaving the bottom to hang free. When they'd finished, the interior of the cabin seemed even smaller, cozier.

Glancing at the bed, Cassie swallowed. A crazy zing of awareness ricocheted through her. Last night, sheer exhaustion had had her sleeping for hours. Tonight, no less fatigued, she doubted she'd close her eyes.

There was something about a real bed, a real mattress that conjured up all sorts of thoughts and memories she'd do well to forget. But for some reason the walls seemed to rush in, cocooning them in intimacy. It was a little disconcerting to find that despite all that had passed between them, the one thing that hadn't lessened was the attraction he held for her.

And the one thing that hadn't changed was the way he felt about her ability.

"Well." His voice sound hoarse. "Makes for early nights."

Nodding jerkily, she said, "Once we got older, Hawk and I suspected that the main reason our parents brought us here is because we were forced to go to sleep when it got dark. There was nothing else to do.''

"Good parenting tip. I'll have to make note of that.''

It was too painful to meet his gaze. But when she would have turned away, he stopped her with one hand on her sleeve. "You asked if I'd reject our child.'' There was a raw kind of hurt in his voice, one she was helpless to erase. "Nothing can prevent me from loving her. All of her. I don't know how to convince you of that. But you have my word. I promise you, Cass.''

She saw the truth in his expression and her eyes misted. It didn't assuage all her fears, but it did reassure her. Their daughter would be completely, totally loved. And when Cassie could no longer be there for the child, she'd still have one parent to keep her world safe and her spirit nurtured.

He crooked a finger, used it to lift her face to his. His lips brushed hers, softly, so softly. They swayed toward each other, her arms finding his shoulders of their own accord before something had them both freezing.

With her senses sluggish, it was a moment before comprehension filtered in.

The pebbles in the cans were rattling. Over and over again.

Chapter 11

For a moment Cassie and Shane both froze. He recovered first, tearing away and switching off the flashlight. Then he strode to the front window, lifted a corner of the rag to peer out. It took a few moments for his vision to adjust to the darkness outside. And when it did, he saw the three pairs of gleaming eyes in front of the cabin. Right in front of the cabin, as a matter of fact.

"What is it?" Cassie's voice was nearly soundless, right at his shoulder.

"We've got visitors, all right. But it's the four-legged kind." Lifting the rag away, he let her look out.

"Raccoons." Her voice was filled with delight. "Most smaller animals would have been startled away, but 'coons are curious creatures."

"And they're messing up my perimeter," he grumbled. "Get rid of them."

Cassie got one of the flashlights and opened the door. "Get out of here! Shoo!" Their unwanted guests turned and scampered away while Shane did a quick circle of the cabin, rifle in hand. They both ducked back into the cabin. She didn't ask if he'd seen anything. She knew that in this darkness, unless someone was standing in full view ten feet away, they might as well be invisible.

The thought sobered her. Shane crossed the room, setting the rifle within easy reach of the bed. Slowly Cassie shut the door, locked it and replaced the chair under the knob. It had been a couple hours since she'd consciously thought of Sheridan and her partner, still out there. Still following them. They'd been at the cabin nearly five hours. That gave their pursuers more time to close the distance between them.

Somehow, throughout their journey, their arrival at the cabin had seemed like a destination. Once they got there she'd hazily imagined being safe with Hawk, the FBI agent and whoever else was in the party her brother would gather.

Instead, they were just as alone in the cabin as they had been walking through the forest. And she knew, deep inside her, that they were on their own.

She took her rifle and carried it over to set it next to Shane's. She'd grown up in this part of the country, and she knew how to handle a gun. If Sheridan managed to find them, she'd discover herself in a whole lot more trouble than she'd ever bargained for.

When she turned again, it was to see that Shane had slipped his coat off, hung it over hers. He pulled a chair out and sat down to unlace his boots.

Slowly, she sat on the edge of the bed and did the

same. "Maybe one of us should keep watch. We could take turns."

"We can afford to rest," Shane said quietly. For some reason, she had the crazy feeling that he knew exactly what she'd been thinking. "That's what the perimeter is for. And thanks to your furry friends, we know that it works. If anyone tries to approach the cabin, we'll be warned."

Still, she was reluctant to lie down. Adrenaline hadn't completely receded, and was now layered over alert hormones and emotions left raw by his earlier words. *I promise you, Cass.*

He approached with the extra blanket, and she moved over, finally stretching out, but hugging the side of the bed. Spreading the blanket over her, he lifted one corner and slipped in, stretched out on his side, facing away from her. Seconds ticked away, melted into minutes. But Cassie knew neither of them relaxed. She could see the tension in his shoulders, in the rigidity of his spine.

Then he gave a deep sigh, moved carefully to his back to avoid bumping her on the narrow bed. "I can't be this close to you and not hold you, Cass. Just that. Nothing more."

Her body flowed toward his, fitting against him in a way that was as natural as breathing. With his arms around her, her face pressed against his chest, she could feel his tight muscles relaxing. One of his hands went to her back and rubbed her spine in a gesture meant to be soothing. Even through her clothes, his touch sparked little flickers of nerves just beneath her skin.

All their differences were still between them. Cassie didn't dodge that reality. But there had always

been more between them. She hadn't slept with
Shane the first time considering music and roses and
happily ever afters. Thoughts of that sort had sprung,
unbidden, as their relationship had deepened. And
now, even knowing as she did just how much kept
them apart, she wanted him. Wanted to feel alive
again, the way she only did in his arms. Wanted to
take him away with her, if only for a time.

Her fingers crept to his chest, flexed there. She
could feel the edges of the tape that held his shoulder
dressing in place. He'd changed it after he bathed.
She'd been aware of that, even while she'd gone to
great effort to avert her gaze. She hadn't offered to
help. It had seemed wiser to avoid proximity with
his half-naked body.

His heart was beating beneath her ear, a low steady
thud. And when she slid her hand down his torso,
across his belly, she heard the exact moment when
its tempo changed.

His hand caught hers. "Cassie?"

She heard the question in the word. She thought
she heard hunger as well.

"Just for tonight," she whispered, nuzzling her
cheek against his shoulder. She wouldn't ask for
more, didn't expect it. Neither of them could predict
what the next day would bring. More than anything
else, she didn't want to think. All she wanted right
now, right here, was this man. And the flames that
could ignite so easily between them, taking them
both on a fiery path to heaven.

"Are you sure?" His voice was raspy, and she
could feel the change in the glide of his palm over
her back that his touch had already turned intimate.

Instead of answering, she tilted her face to fit her

mouth to his. He reached up to cup the back of her head with his palm, keeping her still for the demand of his lips.

Shane shifted her so she was half on her back, and took the kiss deeper. Her intoxicating taste was familiar, and its effect raced through his system like wildfire. Each time he'd touched her it had been like this, he thought hazily, his mouth eating at hers. Wilder. Faster. Hotter than the time before. Like any addiction, his body recognized the source of its obsession and responded instantly. Greedily.

He raised his knee, pressed it between hers. His palm slid lower, cupping and kneading her tight bottom. Her active lifestyle was apparent in the taut muscles there and beneath the silky skin of her thighs. But there was softness, too, a sweet contrast to the strength in the curve of her waist, the mounds of her breasts. Every inch of her was etched on his memory, the places that made her sigh, those that made her moan. He wanted to discover them all again in an endless torment to the senses.

Their tongues tangled, doing heated battle that left both victors. The flannel of his shirt was soft from repeated washings, but it wasn't the texture Cassie was suddenly craving. As their lips twisted together, teeth clashing, she unfastened his buttons, swept her hands in to spread across his chest.

There was instant satisfaction in the sensation. The skin there was sleekly muscled, leaner than she remembered. Harder. Her fingers explored the sharply defined bone and sinew. The light pattern of hair there grew in a perfect vee, and her fingers raked through it as they went on their sensual journey.

The night wrapped around them, shutting out the

rest of the world. The total darkness obscured vision but heightened other senses to razor sharpness. There was the sound of their breathing, already unsteady. The feel of his much harder body pressing hers into the mattress. The heady flavor of him, as it zinged through her body, leaving scorched nerve endings in its wake. And always, always, there were the feelings that could never be banished, no matter what came between them.

He tugged her shirt from her jeans, skated his palm beneath it, and she nearly purred. He had big capable surgeon's hands, the fingers incredibly nimble and dexterous, and her body quivered in anticipation of his touch. She could feel the barely healed scrapes on his palm, from his slide down the slope the day before. His hand first glided across her stomach, then paused, as if to familiarize itself with the very slight mound there. She wasn't showing yet; it would be weeks before she'd need maternity clothes. But she knew he'd detected the slight roundness that was barely discernible.

Cassie held her breath, uncertain of his reaction. But she was unprepared for him to lift his mouth from hers, lower himself in the bed so he could press his lips against her belly. She closed her eyes against the sweetness of the gesture, her fingers threading through his hair. For long moments he worshiped her with the brush of his lips, the caress of his breath against her skin. And she knew, despite what else transpired between them, there'd be a part of her that would always keep this memory tucked away.

Obeying the increasing pressure of her fingers, Shane rose above her, stringing a necklace of kisses from jawline to the rapid pulse point at the base of her throat. He lingered there, inhaling the scent that was uniquely Cassie. He'd never known her to bother with perfume, and if she had he would have resented it for masking that clean, sweet smell. It went to his head faster than any drug, wiping his mind clean. And like any drug, it left him wanting more.

He stripped the shirt from her, then found himself distracted by the curve of her shoulder, the delicate hollows beneath her collarbone. Anticipation had his blood slowing to churn thickly through his veins. And when her body bucked impatiently against his, when her hands would have incited him to move faster, he solved that problem by cuffing them in one of his.

"Shane."

If his name was meant as a protest she shouldn't have breathed the word. Moaned it. It suited him to interpret it as a plea. And he was intent on pleasing them both. He skated his lips over the curves above the top of her bra, felt the slight scratch of its lace against his chin. With his mouth he traced her skin where it swelled over the cups, paused to dip the tip of his tongue in the cleavage between them.

He reached behind her, released the clasp. His pulse began to riot. Shane reveled in twin urges, one to draw out the pleasure, and the other, equally strong, to steep himself in it. He nuzzled her, soft skin encased in ribbons and lace. Taking a nipple between his lips, he suckled her through the fabric, driving them both a little mad.

Cassie writhed beneath him. There was something entirely too vulnerable about her position, both exciting and frustrating at once. She wanted more. Closer, deeper contact with that wicked mouth. And freedom to touch him, to drive him a little mad in return.

He released her then to pull the bra down her arms. Immediately her hands went in search of him, slicking up his sides, finding all the contrasts of ribs and hollows, the sculpted muscles of his biceps, the padded strength of his shoulders.

Shane cupped her breasts in his hands, skated his thumbs over the velvety nipples. They were fuller than he remembered, rounder, another slight change from the pregnancy. His touch gentled at the thought. Mindful of their increased sensitivity, he bent his head to wet one nipple with his tongue, drawing quick damp circles around the areola, before returning to tease the taut bud with lips and teeth.

Cassie's back arched off the mattress as pleasure careened through her. Each dart of his tongue, coupled with his stroking fingers, flung shock waves of pleasure throughout her system. The sensation arrowed downward, made her ache. With each liquid pull of his mouth, her need was whipped a little higher. She needed him inside her, filling her, to relieve the ache that was forming there. And she wanted him aching as well. Until he needed her more than the breath he drew in, until his body was shaking with the strength of his craving for her.

Her fingers flew to his waistband, and with some difficulty she unfastened the button there, drew the zipper down over the hard length straining behind it. "Slow down," he murmured, his hand moving to catch hers. "There's no hurry, is there?"

Her lips curved. "There will be." He'd always tried to set the pace of their lovemaking, taking delight in driving her wild while he'd tempered his own response. He was a man comfortable in choosing his own path. She'd never experienced more pleasure than when she managed to topple him off his charted course.

She rose to her knees, swaying above him. And when his hands would have come to tease, to divert her from her purpose, she evaded them. She pulled his heavy jeans over his hips and down the length of his legs to toss them aside. Then she paused to strip off his socks before climbing up his body again. The chill in the air was more than offset by the heat snapping between them.

"Now you're overdressed," he murmured aggrievedly.

"And you're behind," she teased.

"This isn't a race. Quite the opposite, in fact." The last word was strangled as her fingers walked up his thigh, closed around him.

"Oh, but it is." And this time, she was going to be sure he was first. First to lose himself, until he was drowning in the pleasure she could give him. First to demand the more intimate contact that would drive them both over the edge. First to regret when it was over. First to want again.

She explored the length of him, pulsing velvet over steel. The sound of his ragged breaths was satisfying, each sounding as if it was sawing out of his lungs. But it wasn't enough. Not yet. Her lips brushed the rounded head of his shaft; her tongue licked him delicately. She felt his hands on her shoulders, growing more urgent, and resisted his efforts to draw her up to him. Instead, she kissed and tongued the length of him, set on bringing him the same sort of shattering ecstasy he'd always brought to her. And when she felt his fingers tangle in her hair, heard her name ripped from his throat, she took him in her mouth.

The evidence of his pleasure stoked her own. Cassie reveled in his body's reaction. The muscles of his thighs were tight beneath her, and his hips arched as she took him deeper.

The world had receded, leaving Shane awash in erotic sensation. There was the silky softness of Cassie's hair in his fingers, on his thighs. The wet, hot suction of her mouth, intent on driving him out of his mind. The stroking of her fingers as she explored him. A red haze floated across his closed eyelids, and he felt himself tighten.

Not yet. The single savage thought was more instinctive than conscious. Not now, not without her. He wanted to be inside her, buried to the hilt, and to feel every tremor as the pleasure took them both. He needed to hear those little cries she made when he was thrusting inside her, and the sound of his name on her lips right before their passion exploded.

That need was strong enough to have him evading her efforts to end it now for him, with a shattering release. Easing away from her, he flipped their positions and kissed the protest from her mouth with lips that were just a shade savage. He worked on steeping her in sensation, his mouth going to her breast even as he worked at the fastening of her jeans. There wasn't time to enjoy the scrap of silk encasing her soft mound. Not when his attention was deflected by the dampness that had moistened it. His hands a little too hungry, he shoved the jeans over her rounded hips and off her legs.

Cassie writhed beneath him, one sensation careen-

ing into another. She'd wanted to shred his restraint,
to torch his desire until it equaled hers. Surpassed it.
But the signals of his tattered control had her body
betraying her. If he was impatient, so was she. Her
nails bit into his shoulders as she urged him closer.

Shane skated a hand up her thighs, lingering between them. Her damp heat moistened his fingertips
as they opened her soft folds. He kept one thumb
rubbing rhythmically against the tight bundle of
nerves he'd exposed, while he gently eased another
finger inside her.

His mouth was still tormenting her breast, and the
triple assault drove the breath from her lungs. When
she would have reached for him, would have striven
to snap what was left of his control, he shifted away
from her, then renewed his efforts. A hot ball of need
was fisted in her stomach, expanding with every
brush of his thumb, pull of his lips. He worked his
finger more deeply inside her, and she gave a tortured
cry.

A sheen of perspiration was slicked over them.
Shane welcomed the slight sting of her nails biting
into his shoulders. Her whimpers whipped his passion to fever pitch, torching the remnants of his restraint. Time, which had ceased to exist for a while,
was rapidly spinning out of reach.

Cassie felt him shift, spread her thighs wider. A
moment later his finger was replaced by the rigid
length of his shaft, and he entered her with one long,
sure stroke. The intimate invasion had her back arch-
ing with shock. He felt huge, hard and impossibly
deep, and she writhed, trying to accommodate him.
Then he withdrew a little, and she hauled oxygen into
her strangled lungs before he gripped her bottom in

his hands, tilted her hips upward and thrust more firmly inside her.

Her heart was pounding against the wall of her chest. She could barely make out his face as his body moved above hers. Mind-shattering pleasure tormented her, eluded her grasp, shimmering just out of reach. Her legs wrapped around his thighs, her hips pistoned frantically against his.

With each lunge he buried himself more deeply inside her, took them both a little closer to the edge. Sensation slammed into sensation, each heightening the other. There was the hard wall of his chest, flattening her breasts. Their breaths mingling, ragged and harsh. And the incredible feeling of being filled by him, completely, over and over again.

His hips pistoned, slamming against hers, and abruptly she crested, his name an unconscious cry on her lips. He shuddered in her arms as he thrust again wildly, before going rigid, his body bucking against hers. And in the end, they toppled over the edge together.

Eventually, once they could move again, he turned her to her side, with him pressed behind her back, her sweet bare bottom nestled between his thighs, so he could be facing the door. Because he was reluctant to let go of her, he kept one arm firmly around her waist. Brushing his cheek against the top of her head, he whispered, ''Go to sleep. It's okay.'' Little by little he felt her body go lax. The hand that had been caressing his arm went still.

It was, he thought, a little bit of heaven to hold her like this again. To make love to her, with all the fire and scorching heat that always combusted between them. To lay quietly afterwards once the aftershocks of pleasure had eddied away, leaving this incredible sense of well-being.

But after a time reality nudged at the corners of that feeling. Their situation was no less precarious than it had been in the forest. And without Hawk here with the help he'd promised, it was up to him to keep Cassie safe from Sheridan and whatever the woman had planned for her. He'd faced life-threatening dangers before and come out alive. But he hadn't had Cassie's well-being to worry about then. Hadn't had this anxiety about keeping her and the baby she carried out of harm's way. His greatest fear was failing her, dying and leaving her to a fate he couldn't even imagine. One worse even than the one she imagined for herself.

He thought then about the dream she'd talked about, a sense of fatality evident in her voice. What kind of bravery did it take to face every day, certain their number was predetermined? She'd scoff at him if he said that out loud, but he thought he'd learned a few things about courage. They were all shaped by the choices that they made. But true character was evident in the ways they learned to live with those choices. He was still grappling with that lesson himself.

His fingers splayed softly over her stomach. Medically speaking, he was well aware of every physical step of fetal development. What was new, what had completely blinded him, was the emotion that accompanied the knowledge, knowing his baby grew inside her. He never would have imagined this primal surge of feeling that negated logic, blinded reasoning. Whatever it took, whatever the price, Cassie and the baby would survive this. He would make sure of that. With the resolve came a sense of peace. Gradually, he felt his body relax. And when sleep finally came, and the edges of consciousness receded, it wasn't the future that haunted him. It was the past.

He awakened steeped in pleasure, surrounded by soft, warm woman. His fingers entwined in Cassie's hair as she spread a mantle of soft kisses across his chest. She was sprawled atop him, her warmth and weight as welcome as a gift.

This time was more languorous, with none of the frenzy and all of the sweetness. With the fever quenched, they could savor the slow, lazy buildup to passion. They could tease, with long languid strokes, causing their blood to quicken and their pulses to thrum.

Her mouth was knowing and wicked. It grew eager under his, incited by restless nips and nibbles. With clever, seeking hands, and warm, wet lips, each battled to bring the other to new peaks, one stronger than the last. But even as the pleasure built, sure and strong, there was a timelessness about the moment, as if it would spin, long and lovely, into eternity.

When she straddled him, taking him smoothly inside her, there was a starburst of sensation in his heart. She paused, sighed, as if she'd experienced the same. And then she began moving over him, in a ride designed to drive them both wild. And as she rocked them both to pleasure, his arms wrapped securely around her, he thought of nothing but her.

Cassie lay sprawled on top of him, giving no indication of a desire to move. He wasn't complaining. She was exactly where he wanted her.

They didn't speak. He stroked her hair as he stared into the dark, content to listen to the sound of her soft breathing. One of her hands caressed his chest. Long minutes passed. When she spoke her voice was hushed. ''I was dreaming again, right before I woke up. You were in it.''

Lazily pleased, he looked down at her. ''I think I like your dreams.'' The remark was almost worth the slight pain when she pulled a hair on his chest.

''Not that kind of dream.''

Amusement abruptly vanished. He could feel his chest go tight. ''The same one?''

She shook her head. ''Of you. With our daughter.''

Something inside him eased, just a little.

''She's about two, I think, wearing a frilly yellow dress and black patent leather shoes. You must have bought her the dress. I've always steered clear of yellow.'' There was a smile in her voice. ''You're proud because you've managed to dress her yourself. You're throwing her up in the air, and both of you are laughing.''

Feeling at a loss, he continued to stroke her hair. ''That's good, Cass. That's a nice dream.''

''Her shoes are on the wrong feet.''

That surprised a laugh from him. ''What?''

''You've put her shoes on the wrong feet. You'll need to watch that when she starts walking.''

''I'll try, but I'll probably count on you to correct my many fashion errors.''

There was silence then, and stunned, he recognized what she was thinking. That she wouldn't always be there to teach him how to be a father. That her fate, inescapable, would catch up with her before their daughter could grow to adulthood.

And he was helpless to convince her otherwise. There were no words he could offer that would sway her from her belief, and he didn't want to argue. Not now. So he held his tongue and said nothing at all.

But her voice sounded again, as if she'd plucked the thoughts from his mind. "There's no use railing against things that can't be changed. We have to learn to accept what is, or we can never pick up the pieces and go on."

At first he wasn't sure how to interpret her words. Was she referring to his reaction to her ability again? But then her fingers grazed the bandage on his shoulder, one fingertip tracing the seam it made against his skin. And he knew her meaning had less to do with her, and everything to do with him.

"Tell me." It was whispered, an invitation more than a plea. And no one was more surprised than he when he opened his mouth to do just that.

"It was after the other hostages and I had been freed. A couple weeks or so. Our only ambulance was gone. They'd taken a couple critical patients to Sharan for more intensive care."

The recital, coupled with the stark blackness around them, flung him back to the past, and two thousand miles from here. It had been night then, too. And the danger had been just as palpable. "A missionary from a nearby village reached our clinic and begged us to go back to fetch a young boy I'd treated. He'd had pneumonia, but had seemed to be responding well to antibiotics so we'd let him leave with his mother a couple days earlier. He had a relapse and from the missionary's description he was critical. A couple of us took a jeep and went to get him. The village wasn't far. Ten miles or so.

"It happened on our way back." All his concern at the time had been for the boy. He and the French nurse by his side had done their best to make him comfortable before beginning the ride back. The villager had been right; the child had been gravely ill. "I'm not sure how many of them there were, or what they wanted. Probably the jeep. It was too dark for them to know we were from the clinic. When the shooting started, we both shot back."

But he'd been the one who'd been wounded. The bullet had caught him in the shoulder and toppled him out of the jeep. Davida had stopped the vehicle, while still shooting at the bandits. "One of them wouldn't give up. Maybe he thought I was dead because he came running up to the vehicle." The rest was something of a blur. The searing agony in his shoulder, the breath driving out of him when he hit the ground. The man diving toward the jeep. Toward Davida and the boy. "I tripped him and he dropped his gun. We both went for it. I got there first. I shot him."

"It was self-defense, Shane."

"I didn't have to," he said emotionlessly. He'd analyzed the scene often enough in his mind. He recognized the truth. "I had the gun, his options were limited. You talked about choices earlier. I made mine." As a doctor he'd lost his share of patients on the table. Railed against greedy death for snatching them beyond his help. He would never have imagined choosing death for someone himself. And yet he had. And he couldn't honestly say whether he would make a different choice, if given the chance again.

"What would have happened to that nurse and the boy if you'd been killed? You were wounded. She was driving." With a jolt he recognized she'd described the scene exactly. "If he'd managed to overpower you on the way back, they would have been dead instead of him. Sometimes it isn't about right and wrong. Sometimes it's the lesser of two evils."

"And putting ourselves in the position of deciding which is the lesser evil is a dangerous proposition," he countered.

But she wouldn't be swayed. "Why do you suppose you were spared, Shane?"

He frowned, not following her train of thought.

She went on. "What hand held back the knife that could have ended your life when you were a hostage? How did you survive both that and the gunshot?"

"I don't know." His voice was hoarse. He'd asked himself that very question more times than he could count.

"You don't know," she repeated softly. "And you can't turn to science for a logical explanation. Sometimes you have to rely on faith. There was a reason for your survival. Maybe it's all the good you've yet to do for your patients. Maybe"—here her voice hitched a little—"it's for the daughter you're going to have. It doesn't matter what the reason is. You accept the gift you've been given, and go on."

She went silent, and she said nothing else for a few moments, though he knew she didn't go back to sleep. He recognized that her words could as easily be applied to her as to himself. She didn't question this so-called ability of hers, she accepted it.

But acceptance was a tricky thing, he thought bleakly. It required a suspension of logic, and the search for solutions. That meant turning his back on a lifetime of reason and embracing something else entirely. He wished he could follow her advice. Not only would he make peace with his past, he'd smooth the difficulties between Cassie and him.

It was good advice. He only wished he knew how to take it.

Hours later when his eyes blinked open, he felt momentarily disoriented. An instant later he realized what had awakened him. He was alone in the bed.

Alarmed, he bolted upright, then immediately realized Cassie was still in the cabin. He could hear her rummaging around in one of the packs, and when his eyes adjusted to the dark, he could make out her shadowy form taking something out of it. He heard the telltale crunch and grinned. Cassie's infamous appetite had struck again.

He looked toward the nearest window, wondered what time it was. Fingers of light hadn't slipped around the edges of the rag covering it, but he thought the interior of the cabin seemed lighter. He calculated that it was close to dawn.

There was a thud, then the sound of Cassie's fruit rolling across the floor. "You're busted," he said, lying back on the mattress. "I know you've been raiding the food supply. You could bring me breakfast in bed, but not whatever you just dropped."

There was silence, and he sat up, swinging his legs over the bed. "Cass?"

He saw her still form and swore, leaping across the room toward her. "Easy, baby," he whispered, slipping his arm around her waist. Her pulse was hammering beneath his touch. He didn't try to move her until he felt her slump, the breath streaming out of her. Then he scooped her up and carried her back to the bed to lay her down.

"Here," she muttered, her legs moving restlessly.

"That's right, I'm here," he soothed, pulling the blanket over her. "It's okay now. You're okay."

She reached out and grabbed his arm. "They're here. At the stream." He froze, her words sending ice through his veins. Cassie's voice remained weak, but insistent. "It's Sheridan...the man. They're here."

Chapter 12

For a moment Shane was frozen, doubt and apprehension warring. Then he felt the fierce clutch of Cassie's fingers, and something seemed to click into place. She hadn't been wrong yet. In the end, it was that fact that got him moving.

He fumbled for his clothes, dragged them on. Shoving his feet into his boots, he laced them swiftly, grabbed his coat off of the chair. Walking back toward the bed, he noted that she'd gotten up and was dressing. He retrieved his rifle next to the bed and said, "I want you to stay put and I'll check it out." A cold, tight feeling of dread was already pooling nastily through his chest.

"I'm coming with you."

He tipped her chin up to his, barely able to make out her features in the darkness. "You'll stay here. Close and lock the door after me. Get dressed, have your rifle ready and take up position behind the door.

I'll announce myself when I get back. If anyone else comes through it, shoot them.''

"It'd be better with two of us against two of them,'' she argued fiercely. Already she was half-dressed.

"Hopefully it won't come to that. If it does…'' He leaned down, kissed her hard on the lips. "You have our baby to protect.''

Before she could protest again, he crossed to the door and slipped outside. The sky had lightened, a rosy glow already apparent between the trees. Carefully he picked his way through the sticks they'd planted, stepping over the line strung through the cans. Then he sidled toward a grove of nearby trees, using their cover as he made his way toward the stream.

When he reached it he stopped, watched carefully. One minute stretched into another. And then another. It should have been long enough for adrenaline to seep away. There was nothing to see or hear but the sounds of the forest awakening. There was the trill of a bird. The deep croak of a frog. The buzz of unidentifiable insects.

Shane remained motionless. Nothing would make him happier than to discover that Cassie had been wrong. That Sheridan hadn't found them. But as much as he wanted to, he couldn't quite bring himself to believe it. So he stayed hidden, straining to keep his gaze on the stream.

The figures seemed to appear out of nowhere. Stealthily moving out of a dense area of trees, they approached the stream, close to where he and Cassie had bathed yesterday. One person nudged the other and pointed at the cabin, then both pulled out guns.

Even at this distance he recognized one of the in-
dividuals. It was the man who'd held a gun on them
outside the barn.

Cassie had been right. Sheridan had found them.

Calmly, coldly, he brought the rifle up. Sighted.
Squeezed the trigger.

The shot shattered the quiet. Birds flew squawking
out of the treetops. Sheridan and her partner dived
for cover. His shot had pulled right. Grimly Shane
corrected and sighted again. Of the two of them, he
thought the woman posed the greatest threat to Cassie, so he aimed for her.

Bullets started flying over his head as he squeezed
off another shot. He heard a grunt, hoped he'd hit
something major.

"Go after him, you fool. I'll cover you." It was
the woman's voice. Shane tracked the direction it had
come from and shot again. This time he creased the
clump of bushes she'd taken shelter behind. Shane
rose to a crouch, ran to a nearby tree.

"Hell with that. You go after him," he heard the
male say. For an instant the man popped up, sent off
several shots in the direction he'd just left. It occurred to Shane, in a distant portion of his mind, that
their shots were accompanied with little noise. They
were both using silencers.

It also occurred to him that had he not moved a
moment ago, he'd be dead meat.

Swiftly he calculated. He had ten shots, maybe
twelve total before his clip was empty. The spare
ammunition was still in one of the packs in the cabin.
He'd have to make every bullet count.

He stayed low, edging to the side, keeping the
other two in sight. Only when he saw movement did

he risk a shot, then dive away before they retaliated. He was going to try to circle around them, get at their back. If he was lucky, very very lucky, he wouldn't have an empty clip by the time he got there.

For several minutes things remained silent. He crawled through the cover, straining to see signs of movement across the stream. There was a rustle of leaves, a blur of motion. Quickly he shot then heard a curse.

"There's only one shooting." Sheridan's voice carried in the air toward him. "It's probably the guy. Get rid of him, while I go after the woman. She must be in the cabin."

Shane clenched his jaw, making his way slowly through the vegetation toward them. Something snared his foot, and he kicked viciously before re-alizing his boot had gotten tangled in some saw brush. He put down the rifle for a moment and pulled the gloves out of his pocket, before reaching down to free himself. The thorns on the vine pricked through his gloves before he could get disentangled. Swearing silently, he grabbed the rifle again and moved, keeping a warier eye on the underbrush be-fore he moved toward it.

The stream was twenty feet to his right when he saw a flash of motion. He fired in that direction, darted behind the next pine as several bullets creased the branches that had shielded him just moments be-fore.

When he lifted his head again, he saw Sheridan scrambling across the stream, heading toward the bushes on the other side. Closer to the cabin. Closer to Cassie.

Instinct, fiercely protective, surged. He fired and

she leaped for cover. Screamed. Fell. It happened too fast to know whether he had hit her or not.

The man didn't spare a glance for his partner. He was heading for cover closer to the stream when another shot split the air and sent him rolling. Shane looked up in amazement and realized that his help was coming from the direction of the cabin. Cassie was firing out one of the windows.

"The bushes, Cass, between the stream and the cabin," he yelled. Several shots rang out, one after the other, each kicking up dirt around the area where Sheridan was taking cover.

"Get over here and help me," Sheridan screamed at her partner.

"Fall back," he called. Taking his own advice, he ran backward to another large juniper. Shane's next shot hit his gun hand. His howl of pain was almost as rewarding as the shot itself. Given his relative inexperience with guns, Shane knew the hit had been sheer luck.

It wasn't, however, enough to keep the man from switching hands. Shane's face was in the dirt as bullets rained overhead, one parting the grass not eight inches from his arm. But the man had clearly had enough, at least for the moment. He continued dodging from one tree to another, putting more distance between him and the cabin.

Keeping a wary eye on the direction in which he'd disappeared, Shane called out, "Cass."

"What?"

His mouth kicked up in a grin when he heard her disgruntled tone. Staying put obviously hadn't sat well with her. She'd followed orders this time. Sort of. But he was thankful she'd found a way to assist and keep herself safe while doing it.

"I'm going to bring her out. Hold your fire, but if she moves, shoot her."

"My pleasure."

He hoped the grim satisfaction in her voice would be a warning to the woman. He moved cautiously, keeping a shield of vegetation in front of him. "Throw out your weapon and come out nice and slow."

"I can't. I can't walk. I think I broke my leg."

"That wouldn't keep you from throwing out your gun, would it?"

There was silence for a moment, then a gun was tossed out of the bushes. It tumbled down the slope to land in the brook. "Now you can show yourself."

"I told you, I think I broke my leg." The woman's voice sounded pitiful. "I can't walk."

"Then start crawling," Shane said without sympathy. "Or we'll both start shooting." He hoped it didn't come to that. Getting caught in a crossfire would be as dangerous to him as it would be to the woman.

A minute dragged by. Then another. Keeping his gaze firmly trained on the thicket, he deliberately shot to the right of it. "Cass! Get ready to start shooting."

"All right! All right! I— It's hard to move. You'll have to give me time."

"Lady, you're just about out of time."

She began to crawl out slowly. And by the way she was holding her leg and grimacing, she just might be telling the truth. She'd fallen going across that stream, and he hadn't known if he'd hit her or if she'd slipped. She moved farther out of the bushes and he saw her pants leg. The upper portion of one side was soaked in blood.

She paused, raised herself on her elbows and glared at him as he jumped the brook to come stand beside her. "I need medical attention. I think I was hit before I broke my leg."

"Lucky for you, the doctor's here." He smiled grimly, never lowering his rifle. "Under the circumstances, I can't promise much of a bedside manner."

She groaned loudly, both hands going to her thigh. "Please. You've got to help me."

"You'll have to crawl over to me." He couldn't afford to take his eyes off the woman, but he was only too aware that her partner could still be nearby. He had to make sure he kept cover, all the way back down to the cabin.

Amidst a great deal more moaning, the woman obeyed, making her way inch by inch to the juniper bush he was sheltering behind.

"Move your hands." He lowered his rifle a fraction to study the wound. The blood could be coming from a gunshot or from a fracture. He couldn't examine her out here, but he could discern no signs of bone protruding through her tattered jeans. If it was broken, it might well be a closed break.

"I'm feeling faint," she said in a weak voice. One of her hands edged inside her coat. "I don't know how much longer I can take the pain...."

He had the barrel of his rifle pressed against her forehead by the time she had the second weapon in her hand. The moment spun out crazily, a wave of déjà vu hitting him. "Don't make me choose again," he said softly, watching the hatred twist the woman's features. Past and present blurred. For a moment her face transposed into that of the Afghan bandit. ''I'm pretty sure you'd lose.''

Sullenly the woman set the gun down. Shane kicked it out of the way. Cassie came running around the side of the cabin, her rifle in her hand. ''Keep us covered,'' Shane told her, scanning the forest around them. There was no way of knowing how far her partner had gone. It would be safer to treat her in the cabin. ''I'm going to get her inside.''

Cassie's gaze jerked to his. ''You're going to help her?''

He registered the disbelief in her voice even as he handed her his gun and positioned one of the woman's arms around his shoulder. ''I'm going to help her.''

Cassie cleared a path for him by pulling up some of the sticks so he could get the woman to the cabin. She was leaning heavily on him. Once inside, he half carried her to the bed, laid her down on it. ''Bring me the first-aid kit.''

He divested the woman of her coat and backpack, checking her over carefully for any more hidden weapons. He found nothing, save for the red fanny pack she wore around her waist.

''I need that,'' she protested, making a grab for it. ''I'm diabetic. My insulin is in there.''

He unzipped the pack, looked inside. A cold, deadly rage filled him when he saw two vials inside, and two hypodermic needle syringes, each carefully wrapped. Hawk had warned Cassie about a drug Sheridan's boss had designed, one the woman would try to inject her with. Coldly he stared at the woman. ''Looks like your *insulin* is safe and sound. Should

I give you an injection?'' The flash of fear on the woman's face was its own answer. ''No? Well, how about if I just put it away for safekeeping?''

Cassie returned with the kit. ''When are you going to tend to my leg?'' Sheridan said venomously. ''I'm going to bleed out.''

''That would be too bad.'' Cassie looked down at the woman dispassionately. Her pursuit through the forest had taken a toll on her. She looked older than she had when she'd come to the ranch—was it only two and a half days ago? Her clothes, obviously expensive, were shredded in several places and there were scratches on her face and hands. It occurred to Cassie then, that she herself probably looked no better.

''Cut away her pant leg, will you?'' Shane asked. While Cassie started that, he squatted down and dug through the woman's pack. There was a long hunting knife, insect spray, some men's shirts and socks and a half-full jug of what looked like water. There was also an extra pistol and ammunition.

He stared at that gun, then at the pack. Then he looked at Sheridan. ''Picked up a few things on your way through the forest, huh?''

Cassie looked up from her task, frowned at him. ''What?''

He gestured toward the woman staring stoically at him. ''Remember the meth makers? Something tells me she and her friend happened upon them, too. Somehow I doubt they'd be the type to give up their belongings willingly. Did you kill them?''

Sheridan pressed her lips together, didn't answer. Shane shoved the things back in the pack, save the shirts and water. Then he took the bag with the syringes and set them on the table. Grabbing the things he'd salvaged from the pack, he crossed back to the bed and knelt beside it to examine the woman's leg.

Cassie had the pant leg slit down the front. He dampened one of the shirts, then used the material to wipe the blood away. The bullet had passed all the way through her thigh, he discovered. And she'd been extremely lucky in that it seemed to have missed any major arteries. Using the tweezers from the first-aid kit, he picked out the stray threads from her jeans that had embedded in the entrance wound, then, lacking pressure pads, tripled sterile gauze pads for each side of the wound.

"Hold these in place, will you?" While Cassie did so, he tore the sleeves from the shirt and tied them firmly around the leg to secure the pads. Then he turned his attention to the break. Running his hands over her leg, he paused midway below the knee, probing gently. He didn't need the woman's flinch to recognize he'd found the break. "Looks like both the tibia and fibula." The leg seemed angulated; he checked for a pulse in the foot. Failing to find one, he braced the leg, then quickly pulled it back in alignment.

A strangled scream broke from the woman's lips.

Rechecking and finding a pulse, he said, "That's the worst of it. I'll find something to splint it with. Cass, cut some long strips from that other shirt." Shane rose, scanned the contents of the cabin, spied the broom. He picked it up, then broke the handle over his knee, rebreaking it until he had pieces in the size he needed.

He used the strips of cloth to keep the makeshift splints in place, checking the pulse in her foot after each one he tied to be sure they weren't too tight. Finally, satisfied that he'd done as much as he could, he rocked back on his heels. She wouldn't be going anywhere for a while, that was certain. ''How much adhesive tape do we have left?''

Cassie showed him. He ripped off a long length, rolled the woman to her uninjured side and securely tied her hands behind her back. Then he looked at Cassie. ''I need to get out and take a look around. There's no telling where her buddy went.''

''He's long gone from here,'' the woman said derisively. Her face was white with pain, but her eyes were still venomous. ''Coward. I hope to God he's dinner for a herd of wild boars.''

Shane raised his brows. ''Bloodthirsty. But then, that shouldn't surprise us.''

''Who sent you?'' Cassie's voice was tight. ''What was this all about? Why am I a target?''

Sheridan looked straight ahead, obviously unwilling to answer. ''You're not exactly in a position to be stubborn,'' Shane pointed out. Still she didn't answer. He shook his head, rose. ''Watch her while I take a quick look around, okay?'' Cassie nodded.

Cassie watched him eject the clip from his rifle and load another before heading out the door. The action was an all too stark reminder that the danger wasn't over. Not yet.

''It doesn't matter what happens to me, you know. He'll just send someone else. One way or another he'll find you.''

Cassie turned her head back toward the woman on the bed. The woman who had started all this, had driven her from her home and through the wilderness. And Cassie still didn't know why. Frustration surged. "Who?" She crossed back to the bed. "Who are you working for?"

A crafty smile crossed the woman's face. "You'll find out soon enough when you're delivered to him. He gets what he wants. Always. And this time he'll get both you and the baby."

Shock spiraled through her. "How do you know about that?"

Satisfaction evident in her tone, Sheridan said, "Nothing is safe from him. No one. So enjoy the time you have left." She grimaced. "Next time he's likely to come himself. And he won't fail."

And no matter how much Cassie pressed, the woman would say no more. Finally she stood to pace, anger flooding her. After everything she and Shane had been through, she wanted—no, she *needed*—some answers. What did she have that would make some unknown man take these kinds of risks to have her kidnapped and delivered to him? Why her? And how was it connected to her brother?

Much later, when Shane came back inside, Cassie looked up sharply. He shook his head. "There's no sign of him." He looked toward the bed. "She might be able to predict his whereabouts, though."

"Good luck," Cassie muttered. "She hasn't been too forthcoming so far."

"Really." Shane walked over to Sheridan, his rifle still cradled in his arm. He used the barrel to nudge her a little. "Nothing to say?"

"Go to hell."

He smiled humorlessly, thinking of the events of the past three months or so. "Been there. Done that." He studied her for a time silently. Then he rose, set the rifle against the table and reached for

the fanny pack she'd carried. Glancing back toward
the bed, he noted the woman had come alert. Taking
out one of the vials, he unwrapped it, picked it up to
peer at. "Looks like you came prepared." He removed the protective cap from the needle, stuck it
into the vial, filled the syringe. Then he tapped it
smartly to get rid of the air bubbles.

Sheridan's eyes never left the syringe in his hand.
He crossed to the bed and squatted beside it. "I did
a little time in the toxicology lab when I was in med
school," he said conversationally. He held out the
syringe, pressed the plunger to expel some of the
liquid. When he saw the woman cower away to avoid
contact with it, something settled in his chest, cold
and hard. "People can put together some pretty nasty
stuff. Bet you know all about that, you being a chemist and all." There was a flicker of surprise on the
woman's face before it went carefully blank again.

Shane smiled grimly. "Yeah, we know a few
things. Like your name. Dr. Janet Sheridan, and your
occupation. But we still have all kinds of questions.
Questions that you're going to answer."

"Not a chance."

The woman's bravado faded when Shane pressed
the tip of the needle against the side of her neck. "I
think you will," he said softly. "I really think so."

She was still, her eyes so terrified he knew he was
right. "Who do you work for?" When she didn't
answer right away, his thumb went to the plunger.

"Benedict Payne," she blurted out, her eyes wide
and frantic. "I work for Benedict Payne."

Shane glanced at Cassie, who'd come to stand beside him. She shook her head. He turned his attention

back to the chemist. "She doesn't know him. Who is he?"

"He's a brilliant scientist." A note of something like worship entered her voice. "He has labs all over the world."

"Labs where he creates stuff like this?" He indicated the syringe.

She swallowed. "Yes."

"What is it? How's it work?"

Flicking a look at Cassie, Sheridan wet her lips. "It creates instant addiction for each individual. We engineer it to work with each person's unique DNA, and the result is total mind control."

"She must have stolen some blood samples from the hospital," Cassie put in then. "She knew I was pregnant."

"I'm guessing from your reaction that it's lethal if injected into others," Shane said shrewdly. He didn't need an answer. The woman's reaction said it all. "Why Cassie? How in God's name did Payne manage to settle on her?"

"She's precog," the woman said simply. "Once she's under the influence of this drug, Benedict can force her to use her abilities for any purpose he chooses." Despite the precariousness of her position, she seemed to warm to her topic. "It takes huge amounts of cash to finance this kind of research. Many of his labs have been raided. By controlling Donovan, he has access to stock market tips, which drugs are about to be approved by the FDA...the possibilities are endless."

Cassie was shaking her head, stunned. "No one knows about my ability," she whispered. She looked at Shane. "Just you and Hawk. No one else." But that wasn't quite right either. With a sudden flash of memory she recalled the stranger at the fair who had not only seemed to know about it, but also the pain it had caused her.

Shane was looking just as shocked. ''This doesn't make any sense. That some stranger would hear about Cassie and decide to use her for his own purposes.''

''He's not a stranger,'' the woman responded, a cruel little smile twisting her lips as she looked at Cassie. ''He's her father.''

Chapter 13

The ground seemed to rock beneath Cassie's feet, the blood freezing in her veins. *Her father?* Everything inside her shrank from the word. Al Donovan had been an honest, plainspoken rancher. But he wouldn't be the one this woman was talking of. She'd be referring to her birth father. A man she'd never known. Had rarely thought of.

"You're lying," she said flatly, pushing away from the wall to stalk toward the woman threateningly. "You have to be. I was adopted as an infant. There was no way he could have known anything about me or my ability."

Again the chemist smiled, mockingly. "Couldn't he?"

Bubbles of fury were boiling inside her. Cassie stared at the woman, wanting to smash something. Wanting to smash *her*.

"Hawk must have uncovered this when he was

searching for your birth mother,'' Shane said softly. ''That explains the FBI involvement, too.''

He wanted, more than anything, to go to her and pull her into his arms. The expression on her face sliced at him, made him ache for her the way she had to be hurting. His muscles trembled from the effort it took to remain where he was. She wouldn't want to show any vulnerability in front of Sheridan—he was certain of that much.

She didn't look at him. Couldn't. She didn't want to see if the pity in his voice was reflected on his face. Her birth father, a man she didn't know, was willing to use her, very possibly kill her, to further his own ends. From what the woman said he was nothing more than a glorified drug dealer, with his global labs and designer mixtures. A loathsome criminal who preyed on others to line his own pockets. That was the man she'd come from. For a moment, she was very certain she was going to be sick.

''How much was he paying you to come after her?'' Shane asked harshly.

''A million dollars.''

The number sent her reeling. She braced a hand against the wall, before her knees crumpled.

''Business must be lucrative. How's he financing it if his labs have been raided?'' When she didn't answer, Shane's thumb went toward the plunger threateningly.

''He's got mobile labs,'' the woman blurted out, straining her head away from the needle. ''Several of them. We set up in converted RVs and he changes their locations to avoid the police.''

''A million dollars is enough money to ensure that your partner isn't going to go away quietly.''

"Nearling's long gone," the woman sneered. "He's nothing but hired brawn, without much brain. He doesn't know anything."

Cassie exchanged a look with Shane. The man had stuck with Sheridan this long, coming all the way through the forest. If he was going to cut and run, he probably would have already done so. But if he had any inkling of the kind of money involved, it would provide powerful incentive to stick around.

Shane rose suddenly, walked back to the table and carefully wrapped the syringe with gauze before replacing it in the bag. Catching Cassie's gaze on him, he said, "I don't want you to come near this." He opened his pack, placed it carefully inside, then withdrew another clip for the rifle.

Her throat dry, she nodded. "Where are you going?"

Shane shrugged into his coat, crossed to the door. "I'm going out there after him."

That stupid bitch. That *stupid* bitch.

Jack Nearling leaned against the trunk of a tree, jerked away when thorns poked at him. She'd gone and gotten herself shot and captured. And he couldn't be lucky enough to have the bullet kill her, of course. There'd been blood, but nothing that looked life threatening. Right now she was probably spilling her guts, naming him, as well.

Sweat sheened his brow and he swiped at it with his sleeve. He'd had his share of skirmishes with cops, but nothing that had gotten him serious time. But with charges of attempted kidnapping and murder leveled at him, there was no doubt he'd go away for life. Or close enough to it.

Hands shaking, he withdrew a jug of water from his pack and gulped from it. Nothing would give him greater pleasure than to have killed Sheridan himself. Now he had no choice but to head out of here, maybe to Mexico. But what the hell was he going to live on there? She hadn't paid him yet, and he didn't have enough money to his name to exist for more than a few weeks.

Had he insisted on prepayment, he'd have a cool hundred grand, which would buy him a comfortable life in a new country. He cursed himself for not insisting on the money up-front. It had seemed a pretty easy deal, though, the way Sheridan had explained it. How hard could it be to grab one woman? If only he could have known.

Mentally he tried to calculate how far they'd come from the truck. It was hard to say, because they hadn't gone in a straight line but had zigzagged all over the damn forest tracking these two. And it had been his skills that had helped them out the whole way, he thought aggrievedly. Sheridan hadn't done squat.

It'd probably take him a good two days to reach the vehicle again. Something in him eased as he devised a plan. He'd hidden it well. No one was likely to find it. And he could get out faster than Donovan and the guy could, because he was traveling alone. He could be in the truck and headed across the state line before they ever had a chance to tell anyone about him.

Which solved his problem for getting away, but not for what he was going to do for dough.

Sneakily, the memory of the Donovan woman wormed its way back into his mind. If Sheridan had been willing to pay him a hundred grand for his part in this, what had her boss offered her? A million? Two? Unconsciously, Nearling licked his lips. More money than he'd ever see in his lifetime.

Unless he played his cards right.

He sent a glance back toward the cabin, now obscured by distance and vegetation. He estimated he'd already come a couple miles. If he went back now he could pick the guy off the next time he came out of the house. Just wait in some nearby cover like a sniper and bam!

Or, better yet, he'd wound the man at first and then use him to get Donovan outside. Once he had her he'd off the man, and Sheridan, too, the bitch. Her cell phone back in the truck would surely provide clues on how to contact her boss. And if it didn't, he had a buddy who was a whiz with that sort of thing.

He mulled the idea over, liking it better by the minute. Mexico was going to be a whole lot friendlier with a couple million in his pocket. His mind made up, he took the time to reload his gun. Then he headed back toward the cabin.

Hours later, Shane stripped off his gloves to rub his burning eyes. He'd been working in circles around the cabin, spreading out wider when his search yielded nothing. If he moved out any farther, he wouldn't be able to keep the cabin in sight, and he didn't dare leave it unguarded.

He allowed himself a grim smile. Not that leaving Cassie there with a loaded gun was exactly unguarded. She'd performed magnificently this morning in the shoot-out with Sheridan and her partner.

But then, he hadn't been surprised. His lady had never lacked guts.

There was a quick, vicious twist in his belly when he thought of everything she'd been hit with this afternoon. If Sheridan had been telling the truth, Cassie's own father was threatening her life. The news had to have been devastating, but though it was easy to see her reaction, she'd recovered quickly. He couldn't think of another woman of his acquaintance who would have done as well.

There had been no way to shield her from the cruel news, but his first instinct had been to do just that. She'd always called forth an innate protectiveness from him. The first moment he'd caught a glimpse of that hint of sadness in her eyes he'd wanted, more than was comfortable, to be the one to erase it. If he was honest with himself, that feeling hadn't changed.

None of his feelings for her had changed. Not through the long, traumatic months in Afghanistan. Not during their hair-raising flight through the wilderness. Danger had a way of shifting one's priorities. And his only priority right now was to keep Cassie and their baby safe.

The sounds of the forest surrounded him. The endless call of the birds, the constant drone of the insects. There was an occasional rustle of grass or branches that each time had him swinging around, gun ready. Each time it was a squirrel. A rabbit. A sharp-faced fox. The constant peak and lull of adrenaline was wearing on him.

He tried to think as the other man would—Nearling, the woman had called him. If he'd been willing to work for Sheridan, he wasn't the type to pass up the kind of money her boss was willing to pay for

Cassie. And since the chemist didn't look like the type with wilderness experience, he could only suspect that her partner had supplied that, too. Nearling would be familiar with the environment. More so than Shane. The best time to come after them would be night. Under the cloak of darkness the man could expect to move relatively undetected. But he couldn't know that Cassie and he wouldn't be on the move again, unless he was around here somewhere watching. Waiting.

He looked up, studied the tree next to him. He was bound to get a better view of the area from a height. There was no way to scale the trunk of this one; its lowest branches were a full twenty feet in the air. But once he had the idea, he began walking again, keeping an eye out for a tree suitable for his limited climbing abilities. One with a good view of the cabin. One from which he could pick off the other kidnapper before he could get close to Cassie again.

"How much farther?"

Hawk turned to Liam Brooks, noting the way the man was shifting uncomfortably in the saddle. "Another hour, hour and a half." Looking beyond the man, he assessed the rest of the riders. Although some, like the agent, appeared to be ready for a break from the saddle, all were keeping up.

"Hope like hell you don't get us lost in here." Brooks looked at the trees crowding the trail, and then at the dense vegetation beyond. "This place is kind of creepy, you know?"

"Cassie loves it. I'd much rather kick back on the beach at our place on South Padre, but she'd argue for the cabin, every time."

It was plain from the agent's face that he couldn't fathom her preference. ''Once we get to the cabin, there's no way to get back to the ranch by tonight.''

Although it wasn't a question, Hawk shook his head. ''We'd never make it before dark. We'll have to camp at the cabin, or start back and stop somewhere near the trail overnight.'' Brooks said nothing further, but Hawk knew what he was thinking. They were staking a lot of valuable time on his idea that his sister and Farhold were at the cabin. If he was wrong, they would have wasted nearly two full days. Giving Sheridan forty-eight more hours to get to Cassie.

Jaw clenching, he turned ahead, kneed his horse to urge a faster gait. They were banking everything on Cassie being at the cabin. But he knew his sister. He really believed that this was the spot she'd head to.

He just hoped that by the time they got there it wasn't too late.

Shane's placement in the giant elm yielded a great view of the surrounding area. From his perch he could see the cabin and a good distance around it. Unfortunately, despite its advantages as an aerial view, it lacked comfort. His backside, wedged as it was in the corner provided by a branch and the trunk, had long since gone to sleep.

He shifted the rifle in his grasp and changed positions slightly. Then he froze, hearing something below him. He waited, barely daring to breathe, until he saw the huge buck, with a set of antlers a full four feet wide, step out of the clump of pines to his left.

Releasing his breath in a silent stream, he did another visual scan of the area. A moment later his gaze bounced back to some tall weeds, about forty yards away from the south side of the cabin. Was that a flash of color? Unconsciously he leaned forward for a better view, nearly toppling off his perch in the process. After several long moments he was just about ready to believe he'd been seeing things, when there was an infinitesimal movement again. A flash of dark blue that was there and then gone again.

Nearling had been wearing a dark blue jacket.

Coolly, Shane considered his options. If he shot from here, his chances of hitting the man were limited. He was hardly a sharpshooter. All he'd do was give away his location. He needed to get closer. With his rifle gripped firmly in one hand, Shane began to carefully climb down, keeping his eyes on the spot where he'd seen the man.

At the base of the tree he reassessed. The man was moving slowly but surely toward the cabin. If Shane moved fast, and kept low, he could go around the other side and ambush him. The thought brought a grim smile to his face.

Moving carefully, he picked his way back in the other direction. Every so often he'd stop, get his bearings again. Once he pinpointed the man's position, he'd go on.

Minutes passed, long and nerve-racking. Shane stopped, lying on his belly, attempted to find the man's location. But try as he might, he didn't see anything. No color. No movement. Cursing silently, he waited longer. Still nothing.

Finding a nearby tree, he swung himself up in it, climbing swiftly. He scanned the vicinity in increments. The cabin. The stream. Nearling had disappeared.

After long minutes Shane prepared to get down. He stepped on one branch, grasping the one above him with his free hand to brace himself. Too late he noticed the nest near his hand. There was a swift flurry of movement, and he ducked as a bird flapped toward him, throwing up an arm to shield his face.

And in doing so, he dropped his rifle.

Well, hell. He contemplated the sight of his gun, lying fifteen feet below him, nearly covered by the tall weeds growing around the tree's base. He made his way down another foot. And then another couple.

And then froze, when the man he was seeking appeared, creeping through the trees.

He was a good hundred yards in front of him. Too close for Shane to chance getting down. But he was making his way toward the cabin. If Shane didn't stop him, there'd be nothing between the man and Cassie.

He took the extra clip from his coat pocket, ejected one of the bullets, then tossed it. The man didn't appear to notice. Gritting his teeth, Shane waited until the man was closer and then tried again. The branches made it difficult to complete a throw. He had to attempt a third and fourth time before he was able to clear the branches and hit a nearby tree. He saw the man whirl, crouch down.

They both waited, long excruciating seconds. C'mon, c'mon, Shane silently urged the man. Come over here and investigate. A moment later, Nearling did just that. For a big man, he moved quietly, scanning the area.

He drew closer and closer to Shane's tree. Shane

poised, hoping like hell the man didn't look up, or
didn't spy the rifle as he passed by it.

. His wishes were almost answered. Nearling passed
under the tree, paused, looked around. Shane went
tense, saw the man look down at the weeds.

Shane leaped at the same time the man started to
look up, hitting him in the back of the shoulders and
knocking him to the ground. He heard the gun clatter
away. Both of them slammed into the forest floor,
Nearling's body breaking his fall. They rolled, and
Shane balled a fist, sent it crashing into the man's
face. Nearling hit him with a swift jab to the jaw that
had his ears ringing, then bucked beneath him, his
hands coming up to clasp Shane's throat.

Shane shifted position and slammed a knee into
the man's groin, feeling his hold weaken, but not
break. His oxygen was slowly being cut off. He
reached for his attacker's head, brought it up and
then slammed it against the ground viciously, over
and over. When Nearling's hands fell away, Shane
shook his head, trying to clear it. And then his eyes
widened as he saw the man grasp a nearby rock and
swing it toward his head with brutal force.

Cassie paced from one window to the other. It was
a certain kind of torture to be the one to stay back
and wait, she thought, fear and frustration a tight
tangle inside her. She couldn't see Shane from any
of the windows, couldn't see *anything*. There was
just forest on all sides. And no way to see what might
be hiding in its depths.

Studiously, she avoided looking toward the
woman on the bed. She didn't want to think about
what she'd told her, didn't want to imagine Sheridan

had spoken the truth. She couldn't trust anything the woman said, she told herself stoutly.

But there was a circle of fear, deep inside, that Sheridan was right. She went over the conversations she'd had with her brother since he'd gone to North Carolina. She'd known he was keeping something from her. It was apparent now that he knew all about the man who'd ordered her kidnapping.

Just what else had he discovered on his search? she wondered sickly. How had the man chosen her? How had he even managed to trace her?

She turned from the window, glanced toward the woman on the bed. Benedict Payne, whoever he was, clearly had enough money to buy anything he wanted. *Anyone* he wanted. Sheridan's devotion to the man had been apparent even through her fear as Shane had wielded that syringe.

Global drug empires, mobile labs and what appeared to be an endless army of employees only too willing to do his bidding. That kind of wealth was its own kind of influence. For the first time she let herself consider the woman's warning.

It doesn't matter what happens to me, you know. He'll just send someone else. One way or another he'll find you.

How long would she have to run? How far? A sense of desolation bloomed. Because she didn't fool herself that this thing was close to being over. Until Payne had been captured and put away, this would never be over. Not for her. And not for her baby.

Her hand went to her stomach in an unconscious gesture of protection. If she was right about her daughter's ability, Payne would be just as obsessed with her as he was with Cassie. There was no way she was going to let this madman get his hands on her child.

She thought again of the dream that had recurred since childhood, and this time the dread slicked over her skin, oozed nastily down her spine. Was Payne the nameless, faceless murderer she'd been fearing all these years? Unbeckoned, the details of the dream swarmed into her mind again, this time seeming even closer. More imminent.

Cassie's packing quickly, frantically. Her yellow ruffled sundress flutters as she moves from dresser to suitcase, dropping a jumble of clothes into it. And then she looks up, an expression of terror on her face, listening to a sound that only she can hear.

She sends a quick look toward the half-closed door before grabbing the suitcase, carrying it down the hallway to the living room. A man is already there, clad in dark trousers, white shirt. Slowly he rolls up his sleeves. And though she lifts her chin, nerves show in the way her fingers tighten around the handle of the suitcase.

"Where are they?" the man asks.

She doesn't back down in the face of his angry demand, although she has to be aware of the menace in it.

The pretty Tiffany lamp, with the delicate wisteria winding about the shade, is picked up from a table, sails across the room. When she ducks it shatters against the wall, shards of colored glass spraying like tiny missiles. And then the man lunges, diving for her, and Cassie dodges. He catches the fabric of her dress, yanks her to the couch and his balled fist smashes into her face.

"Where are they?"

The words are uttered in an enraged roar, the blows raining down fierce and punishing. The woman fights, almost breaks free, but his hands go to her throat and squeeze. She claws at them in an attempt to loosen his grip, but his fingers tighten as reason recedes and temper takes over. Her struggles grow weaker, until finally her hands drop away, one palm facing upward in a silent supplication. And then there is no sound in the room but the harsh breathing of the man above her, his guttural, furious cry.

Aspects from the dream melded with the reality of the present. She remembered in her dream there was a child in the closet. But it was a boy. Maybe Shane had been wrong about the sonogram and she was carrying a son. Perhaps that scene from her unconscious heralded her own end, with her child looking on.

Suddenly the air grew too thick to breathe. She leaned against the window jamb, hauling deep breaths into her lungs.

"You look terrified." Sheridan's voice sounded satisfied. "You should be. If you knew what this drug will do to you…"

Cassie straightened her shoulders, turned to look squarely at the woman on the bed. "Benedict failed. *You* failed. And I am never, never going to let him get his hands on me or my baby." She shrugged off the sense of predestination that had dogged her for as long as she could remember. She and Shane outwitted him once, by capturing Sheridan. They could do so again.

But just as quickly she recalled that Shane's part in this was over, just as soon as Nearling was brought in. His agreeing to be a part of their child's life didn't mean he was signing on for an infinite struggle with an international criminal. It wasn't his fight. Neither, really, was this one.

Once again her gaze went to the window. Where *was* he? How much longer was this nerve-racking wait going to take?

"Cassie!"

When she heard her name she almost thought sheer longing had summoned him. Jerking around, she peered outside but saw no one. Without thought, she grabbed her rifle.

"Cassie, are you in there?"

A whirling ball of joy burst in her heart as she recognized Hawk's voice. "Yes, I'm here. I'm safe."

A moment later she saw him running toward the cabin and went to the door to throw it open. "Be careful," she called. "Nearling's still out there." Her words didn't stop his approach. He raced up to the door, through it, grabbing her in his arms and off her feet.

"Thank God, thank God," he repeated, his voice muffled by her hair. "I've been going crazy."

She clung to him, heart in her throat. "What the heck took you so long?" The words started on a laugh, ended on a sob. "I thought you'd be here when we got here."

"Tornadoes." They broke apart, and he shook his head at Cassie's expression. "Don't ask. I was going out of my mind the whole time." His gaze went past her then and instantly hardened. "Sheridan?"

Following the direction of his gaze, Cassie nodded, and in terse sentences described the showdown outside the cabin that morning. "Shane's out there right now,'' she finished, concern sweeping through her all over again. ''He's been gone for hours, hunting for her partner. I haven't heard a sound and I'm really getting worried.''

''We'll find him,'' Hawk said tersely, turning back to the door. Once outside, he gave a wave and a moment later a whole herd of men stepped into the clearing.

''The cavalry,'' she joked, her voice unsteadier than she would have liked.

''Closest thing I could get to it,'' Hawk said. ''Left Jim and a couple of the hands about a quarter mile back with the horses.''

She recognized Frank Lloyd, the sheriff, and a few of the local deputies. The man in the lead reminded her of a taller Shane, with his coloring and air of quiet competence. Hawk introduced him as Liam Brooks, FBI agent. The rest of the introductions were a blur. It was all Cassie could do to provide yet another quick update to Brooks before demanding, impatiently, that they begin the hunt for Shane.

''We figured Nearling would make another attempt,'' she finished. ''From what Sheridan said, there's a lot of money on the line.''

''Okay, we'll pair up, circle the cabin and fan outward. Keep your eyes open and your heads low.'' The group Liam addressed nodded, began to disperse. Cassie gripped her rifle and headed out the door after them.

Hawk jerked her back by grabbing a handful of her shirt. ''Whoa, slow down. You're not going anywhere. Brooks and the others can do this.''

She yanked away from him and lowered her voice threateningly. ''I've been waiting hours for word from Shane. No one is stopping me from looking for him, Hawk. Not even you.''

His face was set in stubborn lines. "Are you nuts? You're the one Nearling wants."

"Then he won't shoot at me, will he?" she asked acerbically. "Don't waste time. You can't stop me."

Evidently seeing the truth of her words on her face, he relented. "Lloyd!" he called out. "One of your men will need to stay with the prisoner. Liam, Cassie and I will go with you."

The man nodded and they started off, the two men flanking Cassie protectively. For once in her life she didn't bristle at the gesture. The only thing on her mind right now was finding Shane. Her palm grew clammy on her rifle. She only hoped they reached him before Nearling did.

Every minute of the search was nerve-racking. When she wanted to scream at the men to move faster, she bit her tongue and kept her gaze sweeping the forest floor before her. They were well away from the cabin now. How far would he have gone?

She turned, squinted toward the cabin. "This is too far," she said surely. "He wouldn't have gone out of eyesight of the cabin." He'd been too worried about her, she remembered with a pang. Worried enough to walk into certain danger for her.

Liam and Hawk exchanged a look. "We'll just go a little farther," the agent said. She knew what he was thinking, and a dart of stark terror struck her. Shane wouldn't have come this far—unless he'd had no choice.

There was a shout from the pair to the right of them, Lloyd and Biwer, one of the deputies. "Brooks! Over here!"

Cassie outpaced both of the men, pushing her way through the clumps of trees, unmindful of the branches scratching her cheeks. She ran as if she had wings on her feet, then faltered to a stop when she saw what the men had discovered. Two bodies, lying at the base of a large tree. Both bleeding. Both unmoving.

Chapter 14

Cassie dropped to her knees beside Shane, her heart in her throat. She didn't spare a glance for the man lying at his side, half over him. Her gaze raked his form frantically, and the amount of blood on his head, on his shirt, stopped the air in her lungs.

Hawk hauled the other man to the side and Liam squatted on the other side of Shane, expertly pressing two fingers to the pulse point in his throat. Then he glanced over at her. "He's alive."

A breath shuddered out of her. With shaking hands, she pushed his coat open, undid the buttons on his shirt. To her relief, she could find very little blood, save for the stain on his bandage. His wound had opened again.

"Chances are, most of the blood isn't his," Liam said quietly. Cassie followed his gaze to the other man, then to Hawk, who was checking for Nearling's pulse. He looked up, shook his head.

Cassie stared at the body, a shudder working through her. That could just as easily have been Shane. The fear she'd felt for him when he'd walked out the door returned tenfold as she realized he'd been embroiled in a fight for his life.

"Hard to tell with all the blood on his face, but I'm guessing from the goose egg on his head, that he got hit with that." Liam pointed at a large rock lying nearby. She swallowed when she saw it was covered with blood. Shane's blood.

"I wish he'd wake up," she said fretfully, lowering her face to brush her cheek against his. She needed to see his eyes open, hear him speak, before she'd be convinced he was all right. Before she'd believe he'd narrowly averted death yet again.

Lloyd and Biwer came up with a blanket and folded it in half, making a pallet of sorts. With Liam's and Hawk's help, they transferred Shane to it, and each man took a corner to carry him back to the cabin.

Cassie stuck to his side, cradling one of his hands in both of hers. She wanted to get that blood wiped off his face. Only then would they be sure of the extent of the damage. There seemed to be a nasty gash above one eye that was still flowing pretty freely. She wondered if any of the party Hawk had brought with him had medical training. As sheriff, surely Lloyd would have some basic knowledge of—

"Cass."

Instantly diverted from her thoughts by that soft

voice, her gaze jerked to Shane, found his eyes open but unfocused. "Shane!" She squeezed his hand, relief doing a quick tumble in her stomach. "Oh, I'm so glad to hear your voice."

His eyes had fluttered shut again. "What happened?"

"We were hoping you could tell us that," her brother said.

There was a slight line between Shane's brows, but he didn't open his eyes. "Hawk's here," she explained tenderly, restraining the urge to push his hair away from his forehead. She was afraid to touch him until she knew just where and how badly he was hurt.

"Yeah, I have to say I've seen you look better, Doc."

Shane's mouth twitched. "It's the beard."

Two of the newcomers that Hawk had introduced as FBI agents passed them, with a couple deputies, heading in the direction they'd just come from. One was carrying blankets and a bag, and Cassie realized they'd be examining the scene and then using the blankets in lieu of a body bag. She couldn't summon an ounce of regret at the thought. Not when it could just as easily have ended very differently.

A makeshift bed was made up for Shane outside the cabin, and once the worst of the blood was washed away, Cassie was relieved to see there were no obvious wounds other than the cut over his eye and the lump on his head. "It'll be your turn to go in for tests this time," she said. "I won't be satisfied until they do one of those scans to check for a fracture or a brain bleed or something."

"Just slap on a couple of those butterfly bandages from the kit and I'll be fine."

Cassie leaned over him, taking an inordinate amount of time to hold the wound closed and to place a strip over it. She was working on the third when Hawk and Liam approached.

"Feeling up for conversation?" the agent asked.

"I'm okay," Shane said quietly. "Nearling?"

"Dead."

He started to nod, winced. "Yeah. I spotted him making his way to the cabin. Headed him off. Dropped my damn rifle so I had to jump him. We fought. He picked up a rock." He stopped, frowned. "Tried to brain me with it, damn near did. I got it away from him and used it."

"That's pretty much how we figured it."

Shane reached for Cassie's hand, entwined their fingers. "Now it's your turn. What the heck went on in North Carolina? Sheridan told us about this Payne guy. She claims he's Cassie's and your father?"

Hawk glanced up quickly at his sister. "God, no, not our father. I'm sorry, Cass, if you thought that."

"Then what is he?" The question exploded from her. "Who is he to us?"

"It's true that he was married to our birth mother when we were conceived. But the files I found indicate that a sperm donor was used. He's nothing to us, sis."

His words brought her a dizzying sensation of relief. The thought of having that man's blood flowing through her veins was overwhelmingly repulsive.

"We've been on Payne's trail for years," Liam

put in quietly. "He's had a long and checkered criminal career, but he made his fortune in the design and sale of experimental drugs."

"Instant addiction," Cassie breathed.

Liam nodded. "He broadened his repertoire with this latest venture. He started out using it for blackmail, forcing his victims to pay him for more drugs. But he had some setbacks. Some of the victims died. A senator, a wealthy French industrialist. And we were getting close. We shut down some of his labs. We're not sure now where he's basing his work."

"Mobile labs," Shane said succinctly. At Liam's startled look, he repeated the conversation they'd had with Sheridan.

"So she's cooperative?"

"She is with one of those syringes against her neck."

The agent's mouth quirked. "I'll keep that in mind when I interrogate her."

Cassie's attention drifted back to Shane. To her critical eye, the gash on his head could use another bandage. But she couldn't bring herself to relinquish her grip on his hand. There was comfort offered in that simple touch. And an intense heat in the gaze he turned on her that infused her with warmth. She reached up with her free hand, fussed with the sterile strips she'd applied.

"We just couldn't figure out how Payne knew about me. Has he kept tabs on us throughout the years?" she asked her brother. The thought of that malevolent presence in the shadows the whole time they were growing up was more than a little creepy.

Hawk looked miserable. "I'm afraid that was my fault. He was determined to keep me from finding the files in North Carolina. He must have overheard me talking to Sheryl about your ability and decided to go after you."

"Mind control," Liam said grimly. "The man's a psychopath, but he's a brilliant psychopath."

Cassie was still puzzling over her brother's words. "Why would he have tried to stop you from finding information on our birth mother?" She saw the glance he exchanged with Liam.

"Because…" He laid a hand on her shoulder. "He killed her." He swallowed convulsively. "He murdered Deanna Payne because she was trying to get away from him. Cassie." His voice went lower, his gaze was intense on hers. "Your dream. The one of you in the yellow dress."

She nodded jerkily.

"I don't think that's you in the dream, Cass. I think…I'm sure it was our mother."

There was a roaring in her ears. "Our…mother?"

Silently, Hawk took a picture from his shirt pocket, handed it to her. Cassie stared down at it dumbly, her thumb tracing the woman's face. Black hair, long enough to hang below her shoulders. Green eyes, fringed with dark lashes. The shape of the face, the tilt of the chin… It was like looking in the mirror.

Shane's voice filled the long silence, anchoring her to the present. "She's beautiful, honey. Just like her daughter."

"I don't understand." Her fingers clutched the picture tightly. "It's always been precog. I've never dreamed of the past.'' A tentative bloom of hope was unfurling inside her. She was afraid to believe it. Afraid to be doomed to disappointment. ''How is that possible?''

''Remember the boy you talked about being in the closet?''

She nodded, her throat tight. Because she'd always felt such a bond with the child, she'd assumed he was hers, or very close to her.

''Because of your dream, I'm wondering if the older children were hiding in the closet.''

''The older children?''

''There's another set of triplets,'' Hawk said. ''They would have been three at the time.''

It was difficult to absorb. She and Hawk had grown up close, thinking they were alone. Then he found out they were actually part of a set of triplets. And now...there were six of them.

''You said the boy had a soft terry toy in his hands.'' Hawk was talking again. ''I wonder if it belonged to you, and if that's why the connection was so strong.''

''That's possible, I guess.'' It was like having her world tilt off its axis. It was disorienting to have something she'd believed her whole life reinterpreted. To be given hope for the future, when she'd never had any.

But it was also a gift. One she'd never imagined receiving.

''Will we meet them?'' She wanted, more than anything, to meet the boy—her brother?—who had figured so large in her life, without ever knowing him at all.

"I'd say that's pretty likely," Liam said. "You all figure in this thing one way or another. And I don't want you to worry. We've gotten some new leads to track down Benedict, and any one of them might crack this case wide open. There was a cell in the truck abandoned by Sheridan and Nearling. I ordered a dump on its records so we might get lucky there." He got to his feet. "Now I'm going to go in and see if I'm as successful as you were getting Sheridan to talk. With more details on those mobile labs, we might be able to nail him sooner than we expected."

Cassie watched him walk away, then looked down at the picture in her hand one more time. Shane reached up to stroke her arm, and the simple gesture soothed her.

"Are you okay, Cassie?" her brother asked.

"I will be." She smiled tremulously. "I really think I will be."

"I'm not a damn invalid." Cassie heard Shane muttering when Sheriff Lloyd suggested he might want to lie down again. Pushing away from the door, where she'd gone to check on Agent Brooks's progress with Sheridan, she approached Shane with a critical eye. His color was better, she was relieved to note. And if surliness was a sign of good health, he was improving rapidly.

"No, you're not," she told him when she reached his side. "When I told Agent Brooks about our adventures, he suggested you might be half cat."

When she sank down next to his blanket, Lloyd didn't seem unhappy to leave Shane to her.

"I don't like cats."

She smiled. "You have something in common with them, though. The way I figure it, you've used up about six lives recently."

He started to laugh, then winced.

"How's the head?"

"Throbbing."

She stroked his jaw tenderly. "I wish you could take something for it."

"Yeah, well, I know enough not to risk pain relievers with a possible concussion. I'll be all right."

"I know something that might cheer you up. I think the group is planning a celebratory feast. They brought real food." She waited a beat. "Summer sausage and apples."

He gave a lopsided smile. "At this point I'm not in the mood to quibble over the menu. I'm just grateful I'm going to get to take part in it."

So was she. She reached out for his hand, needing the contact. Though thankful he'd been returned to her, she knew the hard part was still ahead of them. "I talked to Liam," she blurted out. "About Payne, I mean. He agrees with Sheridan. He won't stop until he finds me. And I can't put the baby in jeopardy."

Shane didn't answer. He just looked at her with a line between his brow that didn't tell her if he was angry, in pain or just puzzled. "He has a place he thinks I can use. Somewhere Payne won't find me. Hopefully it'll just be for a while, until the FBI catches up with him. But...I'll have to leave as soon as we get back to the ranch.''

He was quiet for so long that her stomach sank like a stone. "That's too bad. I was counting on being there with you during the next checkup.''

For the baby, she realized, and tried to smile. This was what she wanted, was more than she'd hoped for when she'd first written him that note. "When I get back, you can be involved as much as you want, I promise.''

"What if I want more?''

The question hung between them, delicate as crystal. Cassie was afraid to answer, afraid to shatter the silence with the wrong word. Surely he couldn't mean what she hoped.

Shane reached out, tenderly tucked a strand of hair over her shoulder. "The way you figured it, I have about three lives left. But I'm only interested in the one I can spend with you. With the three of us. I'm not about to let you go to Liam's safe house, or anywhere else, without me.''

Her heart wept. It was the most cruel torture to have what she most wanted in the world held out to her, and know she couldn't reach for it. "Nothing has changed, Shane. After this, more than ever I realize that. I can't live with a man who rejects part of what makes me who I am. I can handle you not understanding it—''

"Good, because I do *not* pretend to understand it.''

She went on as if he hadn't spoken, "But this

would always be between us. Because of your childhood, your grandmother…''

"You are nothing like my grandmother." His tone
was almost angry. Her gaze flew to his, searching.
"I might have believed that at first, but it didn't take
me long to realize that this ability is real to you."

She looked at the ground. "That's something, at
least."

"That was the start. Do you remember this morning when you told me that Sheridan and Nearling
were at the stream?" At her nod, he said urgently,
"How long was it before I headed out the door,
Cass?"

She frowned, not seeing the relevance. "You left
right away, I guess. As soon as you could get dressed
and get your gun…" She stopped then, comprehension beginning to dawn. And with it a fragile bud of
hope. "You left right away."

"Yes. I wanted you to be wrong, but I never even
thought about not going to check it out." He smiled
crookedly, his heart doing a rapid tattoo in his chest.
"You saved my ass too many times in the last couple
days to ignore your warning. And when they appeared, right where you said they would, well…it
would take someone a lot more pigheaded than me
to ignore that kind of evidence."

"You are big on evidence."

"Right. Because that's part of who I am. Annoying, but there it is." He reached out, traced her jaw
with the tip of his index finger, praying that it wasn't
too late. "I can't even do the noble thing and promise to change. I'll probably always be trying to figure

out the hows and whys of it all. But I can promise that I'll never reject you again.'' His jaw clenched with emotion, his chest expanded with it. ''Not you or the baby. Everything that makes you what you are is precious to me. I love you, Cass. And I want to spend the rest of my life, our lives, proving that to you.''

She linked her arms around his neck and gave him a blinding smile. And he noticed that finally, the lingering sadness had been banished from her eyes. ''I'm not like you scientist types. I don't need proof. I have faith.''

Faith. As their lips met, Shane was willing to admit that even a scientist could use a healthy dose of that, too.

*　*　*　*　*

Don't miss the exciting conclusion to
FAMILY SECRETS: THE NEXT
GENERATION,
when Anthony Caldwell confronts his fate in
IN DESTINY'S SHADOW
by award-winning author Ingrid Weaver

Coming in November 2004
Available wherever
Silhouette Books are sold!

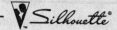

SPECIAL EDITION™

presents

bestselling author

Susan Mallery's

next installment of

Watch how passions flare under the hot desert sun for these rogue sheiks!

THE SHEIK & THE PRINCESS BRIDE

(SSE #1647, available November 2004)

Flight instructor Billie Van Horn's sexy good looks and charming personality blew Prince Jefri away from the moment he met her. Their mutual love burned hot, but when the Prince was suddenly presented with an arranged marriage, Jefri found himself unable to love the woman he had or have the woman he loved. Could Jefri successfully trade tradition for true love?

Available at your favorite retail outlet.

If you enjoyed what you just read,
then we've got an offer you can't resist!

Take 2 bestselling love stories FREE!

Plus get a FREE surprise gift!

Clip this page and mail it to Silhouette Reader Service™

IN U.S.A.	IN CANADA
3010 Walden Ave.	P.O. Box 609
P.O. Box 1867	Fort Erie, Ontario
Buffalo, N.Y. 14240-1867	L2A 5X3

YES! Please send me 2 free Silhouette Intimate Moments® novels and my free surprise gift. After receiving them, if I don't wish to receive anymore, I can return the shipping statement marked cancel. If I don't cancel, I will receive 6 brand-new novels every month, before they're available in stores! In the U.S.A., bill me at the bargain price of $4.24 plus 25¢ shipping and handling per book and applicable sales tax, if any*. In Canada, bill me at the bargain price of $4.99 plus 25¢ shipping and handling per book and applicable taxes**. That's the complete price and a savings of at least 10% off the cover prices—what a great deal! I understand that accepting the 2 free books and gift places me under no obligation ever to buy any books. I can always return a shipment and cancel at any time. Even if I never buy another book from Silhouette, the 2 free books and gift are mine to keep forever.

245 SDN DZ9A
345 SDN DZ9C

Name	(PLEASE PRINT)	
Address	Apt.#	
City	State/Prov.	Zip/Postal Code

Not valid to current Silhouette Intimate Moments® subscribers.

Want to try two free books from another series?
Call 1-800-873-8635 or visit www.morefreebooks.com.

* Terms and prices subject to change without notice. Sales tax applicable in N.Y.
** Canadian residents will be charged applicable provincial taxes and GST.
All orders subject to approval. Offer limited to one per household].
® are registered trademarks owned and used by the trademark owner and or its licensee.

INMOM04R   ©2004 Harlequin Enterprises Limited

INTIMATE MOMENTS™

Presenting a new book

by popular author

LYN STONE

Part of her exciting miniseries

Dangerous.
Deadly.
Desirable.

Under the Gun

(Silhouette Intimate Moments #1330)

After escaping the bullet that killed his twin, Special Agent
Will Griffin awakens from a coma to discover the killer at his
bedside. Thanks to some quick action, he's on the run again.
But this time it's with the one woman—Special Ops Agent
Holly Amberson—whose very proximity makes him feel like
he's under the gun. Because once the assassin
is caught, Will knows his life won't mean
a damn without Holly in it.

Available in November 2004 at your favourite retail outlet

Be sure to look for these earlier titles in the Special Ops miniseries:
Down to the Wire (Silhouette Intimate Moments #1281)
Against the Wall (Silhouette Intimate Moments #1295)